The Red Room

(a portfolio)

Joan Barbara Simon

2

For the seekers

Also by Joan Barbara Simon

Novels:
Long Time Walk on Water (2007)
Mut@tus (2009)

Poetry & Short Stories
Monday Smoothies:
An Anthology of Poetry and Prose
Edited by Joan Barbara Simon (2009)

Children's fiction:
Writing with Pia (2009)

Contents

The Pledge

I try not to feel shame
for any of the thoughts in my head
be they said aloud
or further shrouded
from prudish dissent

Who else but I must
delve into my
unspoken reality?

Not only look
but see which talents
which pleasures
have been given me...

Spring

The vulva -
it's *not* vulgar...
she secretes a juice -

Sebum:

An ooze
of fats,
cholesterol,
some cell waste,
of certain oils,

And it tastes...
try it yourself
if you choose...

Roll your finger in it

Pluck it from your lips with a
smack...

Now, tell me;
you like the taste,
the *feel* of that?

Sebum:

Is a repellent,
it's *not* repugnant...

Keeping urine,
menstrual blood,

keeping those bacteria
that,
if they could,
might flood
the vagina,
away.

Sebum

Is as sweet
as she is kind:

My little army,
keeping invasions at bay.

Favourite Shirt

I want you to wear me
like your favourite shirt;
close to your skin -
for your fingers to linger
on the buttons, on the rims
as you smooth me across your chest
smiling at the mirror to know
how I look best on you.

I want to be that collar
that may kiss your nape all evening -
play with your hair
secretly
as it brushes my mouth and makes me glow
discreetly
in a way that only you and I may know
about lips upon skin upon hair
upon skin...
about limbs...
lost in limbs...

I want to be your favourite shirt in summer
with nothing between us but the odour of our
seasons
you granting me every reason
to saunter where I will;
ride the smoothness of your back
nestle in your armpits
tuck myself in your slacks
hug your waist
as we sit...

I'd get to follow you everywhere
with no-one suspecting
why that smile
plays for more than a while
on your lips as you smooth
again and smooth again
and smooth never enough
that favourite shirt
from the collar

down to my hips.

The Aim of the Game?

Hardly has he entered me but he expels an anguished cry of elation. With the single thrust of penetration, the act was over. Just as I had feared. Just as he had feared.

Kill me!

He hides his face. Why don't you just kill me.

Insuperable shame. Hatred.

Please, just kill me...

I run my hand along his spine, my eyes closed. My body, likewise. My mind searching for what to say in response, and deciding upon silence, for some requests are not amenable to a positive answer.

A day later, we make love again. He is sitting on the edge of the bed as I straddle him. He lasts three or four thrusts. Wait awhile, he breathes-lessly into my face. We'll do it a second time. He thrusts and thrusts, but there is no force behind it. Wait awhile. I need to get a little bit harder. I don't like the position and tell him such. Down on all fours, I spread my legs. Raise my ass. But his soft willy won't stay anywhere. He stuffs himself into me. Slips out. Stuffs himself in again. Wait awhile, he breathes like a man performing hard work, his hips chiselling away at me, but I feel hollow inside.

No!

I pull away. I will *not* wait. You fix your hard-on, then, maybe, we'll try again.

Okay, he husks, rubbing, rubbing himself.

I won't look, but I can hear it, the slosh of his semen, dabbling with my juice.

Just wait a little bit. Just a little bit longer...

He talks to himself, to his penis, like a coach to his team before the match. It doesn't take long for me to detect that change in the quality of his voice. I seize the opportunity to stop his hand, gently, with my own, before, or as it seems to me, he rubs himself raw. There is no recrimination in the language of my touch. It simply lets him know that I know: game over.

Feast

Too much
you ask of me
after the glee
of cake
of wine
to return to dine
on bread
and drink mere water

Blame me not if I therein falter

Not, as I yearn to sup
each your drop
of clear
salty
jewels
of passion
hanging from my lips

My mouth
a cup –
so fill me...

But only cake and wine
only cake and wine

You lay

I dine.

Disclosure

This?

It's not a poem -
a futile clasping
of sensations
that shall leave
without my asking
one day
if I clasp too tight
anyway...

Nor salve to cream the
body of my thoughts
whose limbs
though wrought by whim
are smooth to touch
in self-inflicted pleasures
that I –
endeavouring to deny –
succumb to
in measures...

Rather;
courage to conviction yon mere parley

Rather;
homage

Rather;
unveiled,
my affliction –

This?

Is an attempt
at honesty:
Myself bared
to all
you dare
to see.

Awake

Satisfied to speechlessness
there is nothing left to say
yet the wish remains –
sweet as tortuous…

I love the way you play my ass
my inner eye on yours...
the way you sniff me
read me
mark me as your territory.

What your lips do – to all of mine
how our tongues Sumo
how you wax and polish me with your groin
till I shine, flutter and swoon -

Oh!

Love the pressure of your hands
the right amount at every time
the way you walk
our Bodytalk
the melting of our eyes
your contented yelps of surprise as I
breaststroke your skin, lose myself in
the smell of you, the texture
of you
I cuddle up to
legs and arms plaited like cubs in a den.

I love it
when

you trust me
when
you fall without fear
love the strength of these arms that may hold
you
afloat as the leaves above shake
down
drops
of forgotten rain
to bless our pleasure.

Love our secret power
couched in the shower
of little things that will come
back
to me
again and again
whose collectivity shies naming
but which I feel
full of intensive colour as they call me
now.

No shame

Though a strain of doubt:
Emily...
fool that I am
fool am I to have left her out of my reckoning
certain that she would have matured
to a libertine by now
able to turn a blind eye to my
to our awakening...
I do not want her to suspect me
though she will not be able to stop me

not I, honoured to take
what you give willingly...

No shame:

No space for false feelings
no more two-plane nourishment, for
you make me three:
I swell, succulent with Life
with the unctuous ripeness of possibility
steeped to the elbows
in the inviting ooze of reality...

37°...

salty...

Carmina's Burana (Take One)

Against her better judgement. She sent him a message. A harmless one: she was having lunch with the children and would plough her way through some work in the afternoon. She was hoping he would invite her to come over. She was hoping and yet it was what she feared the most. She waited... but in the end she brought the girls back to school and drove home. Yes. It was better that way.

Her phone rang. He said he had the afternoon free and thought she meant she was spending the afternoon with the children. So, she's not? So, she's at home? So was he and he didn't have any plans for another two hours. He did not ask her to come.

- Can I come?
- Yes.
- I'm on my way.

They sat in the kitchen and talked as her hand never left his thigh. One tea bag served the both of them. They chatted. And kissed. They had less than an hour and the hour was spent to the full in each other's company without the implication of further intimacy. He gave her a CD. As she light-footed into her car and drove down the pathway, Carmina felt senselessly happy.

She sat in her room, trying to resist the temptation to write to him, to contact him. She opened one, two bottles of wine and downed them. She wanted to live the feeling of being in love; that which makes the world go round. She wanted to love him; his freedom, his pride, this glorious and threatening man she orbited round as though warming up to a dare. She wanted to contaminate herself with the freedom he accorded, knew she was of a similar spirit, yet she fell short, guilt like a nail pushing up through her shoe.

Her attention kept being drawn to the place her thighs met. She couldn't breathe. Lost command of her senses. She squeezed her hand to that troublesome place. Felt it throb. Brought her fingers to her nose... sighed.

She fucked her mattress every night she found herself alone. Fucked the walls, the door edge, the table corner, the chair. Anything that was hard enough. Or near enough.

Carmina's ovulations were a ferocious affair. They blocked everything else from view with their white anger, like the child kicking over all her building blocks, the tears searing her face, her voice muddied by the rage that had gathered in a sudden black cloud on a blue sky; brooding and inconsolable.
When Carmina had her ovulation, she hated men. Hated the men who were absent or inaccessible;
the men who incompetent
every lover who had ever loved her
good and bad alike
and who had ever left her.
She hated every man who had shied away from her advances, fear and mockery dancing in their contorted smiles as their feet yanked them back to the cowardly comfort of the commonplace; to the wife no longer loved, but who would always be there, unscandalous. Scentless.

Ovulations meant hate
meant hunger
meant animal
meant howling
meant denying
meant yearning
meant curled up and crying
meant not defying you are ...
Woman

Ovulation meant donation
meant benediction
meant confirmation of your
woman –
recumbent
resplendent
releasing;

a feasting of womanhood

He fell asleep... in her mouth. He had worked her
to a froth then left her there. I can't anymore, he had said,
I just can't. Carmina had thrashed out with her limbs and
screamed till the fury abated into the irregular throbs of a
wounded cry. Sssh, I'm sorry, I just can't, he rolled onto
his back. Ssshh... here. He cupped her head and eased it
down... She suckled and cooed like an infant, a mouthful,
her hand full as he drifted to sleep...
She loved the brown fluff burrowing from his navel
to his groin. She loved his toenails. When she kissed his
behind, he apologised for not having shaven back there.
Don't, she says. I like it that way; his hairy little rosetta
that peeps at her as he straddles her to bury his head

between her thighs. She licks everything that her tongue can reach. Nothing she can do will shock him. This gives her the courage to shed her shame.

I watched his belly rose
and fell
as I teethed his stave.
As I circled his crown with my tongue.
He had taken me
from the front,
from behind...
Had plucked my tampon out and fucked me till I swooned
to the floor
so that he'd had to carry
me
to the bedroom.

Now he reposed as she pampered his softness, as her gaze ruffled his body hair, or wandered in and out of his nostrils. Dark, scentless balls, soft in her grateful hands. Love juice smeared on her brown skin, quiet now, inside her translucent gown that bakes in the sun till he will rise and brush the shattered crystals from her, his lips tweaked by pride. Look at that, he had said. Millions and millions of Tatar. If I were ten years younger I would make you a baby. A beautiful brown boy. He scratched his proteined icing from her nipples, from her neck, her ear. From her chin. His eyes, mellow as he parted her lips with his finger. Mellower, as her tongue pulled against him. Closed, with his eyelids simmering, as their tongues wrestled his finger from her mouth to his...

from his to mine...

... fluttering around the maypole to the melody of saliva, of sighs. Now, he slept. His chest, a barrel of gunpowder Carmina moulded herself against so that his sonorous voice may illuminate her thickly.

With my head on his brown down, and my palms
gliding up,
gliding down the
smooth
inside of his thighs,
I listen to the gargle
under his skin,
kicking
at my ears like a perky foetus.

Tatar had a certain weight which he wore well, above the still slim legs of a younger man. It is unfair that men get to keep their legs. He reminded her of a newborn child, of a tadpole. And she wanted every gram of him. She hugged his mid-drift like a best friend, caressing it as they talked. It slapped her thighs as she rode him, receded in redolent waves that thumped the mattress. Along with his back, it was the part of him she liked to touch the most. It was not the fat of bad nutrition or a want of respect for the body's need of exercise. Rather, it was the trophy of his Epicurean esprit. Carmina accepted its donation of warmth and security gladly.

I suppose I should be struggling with remorse?
Instead, the gargling of your stomach nibbles
at my ear,
your exhalations
bless me as I curl
up
on this
man I should not love,
in a bed that is not mine
yet feels like home,
asking myself no further questions, for it is spring;
the sun pours its yellow cream over my skin.

*

-Tell me something?
-Shoot.
-You said you always have at least two women, right?
-Correct.
-So, there must have been another woman apart from your wife before you met me, right?
(He smiles)
-Where is she now? What happened to her?
-I saw her yesterday, we went flying and then for a meal...
-You don't sleep with her anymore?
-Nope.
-And you expect me to believe that?
-Yep. I'll show you a picture of her. (He shows her a photo of her in his cell-phone) and there's her... (a different photo) and her... and she's nice... and I really like this one...
-How do you manage?
-What?
-To juggle so many women?
-Piece a cake.
-God, you don't mind admitting all of this to me?
-Why should I?
-Does your wife know?
-Why should She?

I, Tatar, am faithful of the heart, if not of the body. Don't try to change me. It is my only weakness.

There is an enormous latent aggressiveness in me. That's why I have always avoided getting into fights. I could kill someone. My opponent would have to kill me, cos if I got the first punch in, I swear, I'd kill him. They can say whatever they want about me: You, you're a fat fucker. I'd say, you're right, I'm a fat fucker, then I'd go about my business. For their sake. You see my voice? I can roar until the walls tremble. I can kill you with my words. My verbal aggression is perhaps even worse than my physical aggression. It's in me, and I know. When I shout, the curtains flutter. My paintings jump away from the walls and a glass will explode into a thousand fossilised teardrops clutching at the strips of light to get away from me.

Some people think I'm stuck up; think I think I'm clever. Well, I am. I'm exceptional. I'll leave the rest of you to be ordinary.

Fidelity is an illusion. I have always cheated on my wives, and they have all cheated on me. Women lie. Men lie. That's life. I am very faithful, but not as far as sex goes. Sex is part of life and it's as natural as breathing. Don't ruin it with false morals or too much thinking. I need sex. I always will. Sex is like a good glass of wine. Nothing more. It's there to do you good. Our bodies are there to do us good, and every single part of our anatomy serves this purpose.

I said I would never live with another woman cos they're all too complicated and things always turn sour in the end. I have been married three times; I know what I'm talking about. I want a woman? I have a phonebook full of women. I can have a dozen different women a day if I wanted to. Women come. Women go.
- Yet despite everything, Tatar, you need one who will stay...

No, honey, that's not true. I'm not seeing any besides you. I can't keep up the pace anymore. It's too much hard work. We were at it last night, then again this morning till eleven. When She comes home from work, She'll want it again. I don't have the time for anyone else.

Don't get attached, for I will not love you. I don't love anyone, apart from my children. Women have broken my heart too often, I refuse to love any of you. Any more...

I can swear anything you want me to: on the head of my children or my mother or put my hand the bloody Bible if anyone asks me to swear to something, what do I care, I'm not a believer. But if I give you my promise... ah! My promise...

These are your best days, Carmina. Live them to the full. I see my ex-wives and loads of women over fifty, they still have the desire, but their best days are done. I even give my ex-wives tips on how to pull a bloke on the internet cos they don't know how and it gets harder the older you get as a woman. You, you are in your prime. Live without regret.

-I don't want to get involved in your private affairs, but you've pulled me in so I'll speak my mind. Have you told You Know straight to the face that he's a lousy lay? You should've told him from day one that he was lousy. He might have made more of an effort.
-He's making an effort now...
-Too late. He's lost you.
-I'm inclined to think that there's a woman out there, somewhere, who wants exactly what he's giving. But that woman sure as hell ain't me.
-Then get out of it!
-You're not just with someone for the sex!
-What else?
-Well, for the companionship, etc...
-Get yourself a dog. Companionship, fair enough, but without the sex, your relationship is dead. It's just friendship. Sooner or later you'll leave him. And he knows

it. He should start looking around for a mistress now, so that the blow won't come so hard.

I made the mistake of telling my wives about my mistresses, you know, in a moment of trust, like this one now. It spoilt everything afterwards and they always threw it back in my face. Don't ever tell You Know about me. Ever. Maybe he's keeping a mistress, too. Or he should. That way you get to save your life together and enjoy those bits of your relationship which do you good. If he lets you know or you let him know, then the trust is out the door. You need trust if a relationship is going to work. Trust is more important than honesty.

Very few people have conquered my heart. Some have tried to get to know me, but have given up after a year or two. I have let some into the antechambers of my heart. They thought they were in the middle, but they were really only in the antechamber. I regret, now, the way I behaved by letting some think they were in, when they never really were. I regret that.

My wife is beginning to pull her hair out. She wants me to go and see a doctor because I can't get a hard on. Not with Her (smile...). I think about you day and night... Do me a favour, when you know that you are coming to see me, don't wash. Try not to, for at least two days. I like it that way; the smell of your *foufounette* nice and strong...

I say the truth but most people would rather hear lies. Don't lie to me, bébé. I want you to always, always, tell me the truth.

He hadn't made the bed, for which he apologised, but it didn't bother her. She trampled on Her blue

28

sequined slippers as she climbed in and trampled on them once again as she climbed out, not that she had anything against Her, they were just in the way. Sex was good, and though she came several times and got the chance to scream her head off, her passion was shushed by a sadness she didn't quite know where it came from, or where to put it, so she tried to stuff it into the crease of cloth between the two mattresses with her big toe right foot. All the sperm She had not been able to summon splattered all over the sheets now. As he creamed her torso with it, lamenting all the millions who had got away, Carmina realised she was lying on Her side of the bed, wondered if Her nose was good enough to pick up the spunk and sweat deposited in Her absence. He fed her a clump of it with his forefinger, so she could taste it, properly, not like the last time, when he had exploded into the back of her throat and it was slung directly to her stomach lining, choking her along the way. She twirled it around in her mouth trying to think what it reminded her of. He would give her everything. He would give her everything! He wanted to give her a wonderful present he was just thinking what it might be. If he had one hundred thousand euros he would give it to her on the spot. Maybe he would even marry her one day.

Would I marry you?

She thought about the sequined slippers she had trampled on. If beauty were celestial and came looking for us under the mantel of darkness, the wife would be the one to hold the candle without the wick, where had she heard that or something similar? And suddenly Carmina knew why she was so sad some place so soon on into this Wonderful: cos although she had laid herself bare, he didn't believe a word she said.

*

The first thing She does when She gets in is to check the sheets. For stains. For ruffles. The first thing I do once my ladylove leaves is to do the sheets. Pull them straight, or at least Her side, and maybe leave the bed unmade so it looks as if I've just got up. I keep my ladylove on my side of the mattress. Get her not to wear any strong perfumes or creams and that stuff. I want to smell you, not some high-tech lab that lines its pockets with all your female complexes. She'll check the sheets. I've been loving and lying for decades, so let Her.

- We're too similar. We couldn't live in the same space, that'd be terrible. We'd end up beating each other up, for we both have a great potential for violence, you and I...
- Me, no I don't!
- Oh yes you do, Carmina. I can feel the tension between you and You Know that you are not even able to retain behind the wall of your teeth when you talk about the two of you. It pours out of you like a gas. It is purely thanks to your decent upbringing that you two desist from bashing each other. And it's all to do with sex. Sex is the most destructive, the most creative force in the world. And I, I spread the good news, like Jesus. I say Love, but nobody wants to listen. I threaten them, their old established values that they blindly hang on to like a flea on the backside of some beast. I threaten their world order. People are so afraid of change I am amazed we've even made it so far. And in their fear, they will lash out and crucify me. Blot out my light with their broad reproachful shoulders, flagellate those whom I have redeemed till they bend, till they bow, unable to seek solace in a promised land, which is none other than this one. Right here. Right now. I must die. And you, you, too, will kill me. One day.

You and your goddamn hang ups! You need to get rid of all that excess baggage and get in touch with yourself.

He kissed the corners of her lips so that her spine whipjacked. Breakdanced. He held her head in his hands like a big sea shell borne high for admiration; for your eyes to pour into the crevices of, like the wind, soliciting deep music.

Your values are all wrong and you can see it cos they're not making you happy. You're sacrificing yourself. For what and for whom? You're not balanced, isn't that telling you something? Look at your face. Don't bring that melancholy into my house. When you are here, I want to- that's better, see, you radiate! Your eyes are like an opened book, so easy to read...

I am God. God is man. Every single one of us is god. If I were god, I would do things exactly as he did, concerning us humans. I would make a man and a woman. Like him, I would make the man strong. And stupid. And the woman weak. But intelligent. Yeah yeah! If it were the other way round, strong intelligent women and weak stupid men, we'd have no chance of survival. You'd have us on a leash and lead us around like a pack of hounds. The way things stand, we have the force to keep you in your place, ha-ha-ha. Haaa-ha-ha!

- I can't be bothered to run after life any more. Right up to my mid fifties, I was panting after life like every one else. Now, I do what I want. Sleep when I want. Eat when I want. Drink when I want...I stand above life and its fretfulness; what's the point?
-That's very wise, what you're saying...

I dunno bout that. There are very few things I need in life now. And one of them is you.

You start off with two fingers, then three. Add, carefully, the fourth, keeping your fingertips pressed together, tightly, in a cone. Ease your thumb in between your ring and middle finger. Withdraw a little. Advance a bit further than the last time. Withdraw. Advance. Slowly... Insist... Insist until the whole hand is inside. Yaaaaa.....

The innocence, the joy, the fear of discovery. Too many had told her why she should not do-think-say-ask-try the things she did-thought-said-asked and tried.
Fuck you all.
Fuck all of you!!!
My life.

My way.

-Open it.
-What is it?
-Just open it.
He shook the box: light...
She smiled.
-No! Don't open it until I've gone.

-And?
She grinned at him three days later.
-I made a blood sausage with it. Blood sausage with horse chestnuts. Delicious!
-You're a swine!

-So are you. You're just beginning to discover your true tendencies. I'm the gardener, getting rid of all the weeds so that the beautiful flowers may take air and bloom.

- Many women fantasize about being raped. I know it, cos more than one girlfriend has confessed this to me. One girl kept going on and on about it. This was at the time of Christine. She was coming to spend the weekend with me. Christine was off somewhere. So, she wanted to be raped? The minute she got through the door, I whacked her full in the face, with my entire force; me a strapping bloke who'd lift 300kg just like that. She spun through the room and fell to the floor. I grabbed her by the hair and dragged her through to the bedroom. She was screaming and crying by now, not knowing what the hell was going on. I beat her up, tied her to the bed, tore her clothes off her. She was screaming and pleading, and got a few more fistfuls for her trouble. I got a cucumber and rammed it up her arse as hard as I could, then I left her there. Walked out of the house and came back a few hours later. She had pissed herself and shat all over the bed. I gave her a second going over and then ditched her there, still tied up like an animal. This went on for 24 hours. She wanted to be raped, didn't she? Don't you, but what you imagine is some kind of friendly rape, where you say no a few times and he forces you just a little bit, cos really you want to after all. That's not rape. Being raped is not nice. It's not nice at all, and I bet I drummed that one fantasy out of her. When you asked me if I had ever raped a woman, you let on that this is one of your fantasies as well. Well, there is no such thing as a nice rape. And now I can tell from your eyes that you regret having asked me and that you're afraid I might drum this out of you, too. Aren't you?

33

- Did it turn you on?

You are a real goddess. I swear, you're not just a mistress or a bit on the side. There is no word to describe you. I shall have to invent one. A real goddess. I am the false god...

-I'm afraid of changing, of no longer being me...
-Maybe you'll finally become the real you, have you thought about that? Maybe you've been living a lie till now, and you're afraid to face the real you...

I don't pussyfoot around. When it's over, it's over. Bam. What is the point of protracted suffering? Ciao. Over.

When I think of you, I don't want to be cooped up in these four walls. I want to be outside. To yell. To be free... To hear nature's applause and thank my body for everything it bestows upon me. I am alive! I am a woman.
Why wait for the big war? Every day is a war, Tatar. War with myself; my reason, my passion...

If you don't question, you slow down, like water molecules before they turn to ice:
you fossilise.
Fossils are dead life...
You think I am the love of your life, but I'm not. He is still to come. Oh come on, spare me that soppy look; it's the truth, and you know it. You'll meet someone ten times what I am. I'm too old for you. I have a terrible past. I'm not the man you want... I'd like to be able to say that I knew you. One day you'll be really famous. You'll travel the world and everyone will want to know you. One time

you'll be in Morocco, and you'll pass an old man, begging in the streets. He'll be seated, cross-legged, white hair, unshaved. But his eyes, his eyes will still be the same old eyes. He'll remind you of someone, and so you'll put some coins in his hand as you walk by. He'll look up at you, and thank you:

'Thank you, Carmina'...

I'd like to end my days in the desert. Just stand still, and dehydrate till I become a stone once more...

Till today he was full of threats should she two-time him. Till today he had threatened to kill her, to shoot her in her knees. He opened his eyes wide as he spoke, as the corners of his mouth pinched the words cruelly on their backs as they tumbled out. Till today. Today they spent the whole morning in bed. Just caressing. Just confessing their passion with the satisfied entanglement of their limbs; the embrace of their ripe eyes. Today, he confessed: there will be others. You will find men who are better lovers than I am. They will swarm around you. Just be careful. Make sure you use protection. And come back and tell me everything. Everything.

He spoke in the present tense of his female encounters. She corrected him to the simple past.

An exchange of glances.

A smile.

A touch.

She cuddled closer and let him talk on.

-I've been thinking about how best to manage this thing we have, Tatar...

-Oh, no, here we go. Don't you know that, One, you can't manage it, and Two, the minute you think you can or have to, that is the point from which everything goes downhill. Don't try to manage, to control – just live!

He kisses her lips hard. Sucks them into his mouth as he slips his hand inside her top to play with her nipples. Her body erupts to the invitation, but each time he gets up and leaves her cold.

-See, we yearn for each other, but you can't control it. And you can't control me. Just live.

-You haven't quite picked up my angle. You're going too fast for me, Tatar. I don't want to sleep around or have group sex. I want a lover. I want to discover. Be discovered. I want sex. Safe sex. I should always tell you the truth? I have come to say goodbye. I can't come here anymore, because I am not strong enough to be myself in your presence. Goodbye. Goodbye, goodbye... kiss me... I can't. I can't! I believe you, I believe you love me, but I can't... I just can't... why do you want to change me?

-I haven't changed you! How can you change someone as quickly as that? One day you won't need me anymore, Carmina. The words crumbled from his lips. I'm just a palliative. You will move on. And I will die. On the inside.

Your problem is that you don't love anyone. Not your wives, or the other women, not your children, not your father, your brother. Not me. Not even yourself. That's why you'll never be happy. You are damning of everyone's slightest fault. You say happiness is the accumulation of little moments of happiness, but if this were so, you would be the happiest man on earth, which you evidently are not. You consume women, not in the search of happiness, but to escape your loneliness. Their adoration feeds your ego, because without it, you feel empty. You keep making the same mistakes, so you stay on that roundabout. The only person I have never heard you say a sharp word about is your mother.

My mother was a lying bitch. She told us a load of bollocks, which we, as children, believed. Looking back, I now I know it was a load of bollocks and that she was a lying bitch. She would go out at night all the time, to meet her lover. The same lover for forty years, instead of bringing him home to be our father. I would have liked to have had a father.
- Maybe he didn't want to be father to you, he just wanted her... mmmh?

A ruthless man, am I? Do you like opera? I do. One of my favourite operas is Puccini's *La Bohème*. Have you seen it? I've seen it on three separate occasions. The first time I saw it, when it got to the part where the heroine is killed, I was so taken into the plot that I just keeled over and fainted. Bam! The second time I went to see it, I thought I was better prepared. I thought I'd brace myself when it got to that part of the plot. When it got to that part of the plot, I don't know, I just felt myself sliding off my chair; slowly, slowly, till I crumpled to the floor. Out again! The next time I went to see *La Bohème*, I thought I would be immune. I knew what was coming, and when, so I was in complete control. My auntie's fanny, was I. They carried me out on a stretcher. There will, alas, be no fourth encounter between myself and Puccini, for I am everything but the ruthless man I am said to be...

*

I can't I can't I can't! Let me go! Let me go, Tatar! You're hurting me! Let me go! Open that door. Open that door right now! Right- No! No, don't! *Don't!*

Carmina's Burana (Takes Two...)

I am Carmina

Carmina is my name
I am as I am
And it's right that way.

I am here as a healer
To kiss shielded wounds
That recede with a swoon
Once their truths have been yielded.

I'm not in it for me
But in it for you
So you'll grow
To know all of yourself
It's your due.

I am as I am
I'm made that way
What more do you want
What more must I say:

I am strong
I am proud
I am dark of hue
So you think you can fathom me
But I'll never subdue
To Man's sway:

For I have my own:
You can't take it away.

I am as I am
And it's right that way
Sick n tired of men
Who don't tire of saying
You're too much of this
You're too much of that -
It's my mind they are trying to kill
Don't you find?

If you're not up to scratch
Get the hell off my back
And peddle elsewhere
That conjugal crap.

Find some Barbie
Big-boobied and blonde
With a hole in her head
And her thoughts
Just on bed.

I am as I am
I surely ain't lying
Not your type?
Then, g'day
And you won't see me crying.

I'm not here to give pleasure
My goal is to dive
For the truths of life
Be they ugly

Or kind.

I am as I am
Been that way for ages
Have the courage to dive:
Just keep flicking these pages.

*

I?
Am Tatar
Tatar is my name.
I am as I am
I'm made that way.
What more do you want
What more must I say?

I'm a democrat. Every one can have an opinion, but if you're working with me, you have to do as I say. One person has to be the chief. I was born a chief. That was clear to me by the time I was six. I know you said that, maybe, that was why my father needed to die so young; to leave me the space and to avoid the competition, but you're wrong. He had to die so young because I would have killed the violent bastard otherwise, I swear. There is an enormous latent aggressiveness in me. That's why I have always avoided getting into fights. I could kill someone. My opponent would have to kill me, cos if I got the first punch in, I swear, I'd kill him. They can say whatever they want about me: Tatar, you're a fat fucker. I'd say, you're right, I'm a fat fucker, then I'd go about my business. For their sake. You see my voice? I can roar... until the walls tremble. I can kill you with my words. My verbal aggression is perhaps even worse than my physical aggression. It's in me. And I know. My father was a bastard. A violent bastard. He would hit my mother, and he hit my brother and me, too. Once, when I was six...

The boy in the shorts, the belt, the screams, the lash, the fury, the father, the belt, the boy, the lash, the father, bulbous eyes bursting to beat the truth out of the boy on the commode, the belt, the screams,

"It was not me and it was not me however you may beat me..."

The sweat, the tears, the lash, the crash, the thrash, the mash of sweat on the belt on the tears on the boy on the commode,

the mother...

the belt, on the mother, on the boy, on the mother, on the boy on the commode, on the mother fallen to the floor with her hands round her head, round the sweat, the tears, the lash, the crash, the thrash, the mash of sweat on the belt on the tears of the boy on the commode, of the mother at the feet of the boy who insists...

"It was not me, however you beat me..."

Leather nailed to their skins, lacerating moments. Looping the venerable swirl of a fly-fisher: Father, wide-legged, up to his knees in the blood, in sweat, in the salt of his fury; of their defencelessness. The sweat that turned to blood that turned to water that turned to the wine of the blood of Christ the boy was being taught to honour: to love thy father, for thy father loves thee, his lamb...

rip
nail
rip

41

nail

the hurt stacked high like dirty dishes, like the corpses in a common, still uncovered grave, fresh insult congealing atop old. The stench courted by the wind, cavorted away so the two may play, may forget the boy, the tears, the mother, the tears. The shame. The rage. The hate.

If he had lived, I would've killed him, driven him to his knees to beg my pardon, or even driven him to suicide. Nothing that is dear to me comes from him. His only legacy was this violence in me. When I shout, the walls tremble, the curtains flutter. My paintings jump away from the walls and a glass will explode into a thousand fossilised teardrops clutching at the strips of light to get away from me.

I am Tatar

Tatar is my name
I am as I am
I'm made that way
If I desire to laugh
Then I'll laugh till I sway
I love those who love me
Though it's no fault of mine
If it's not the same person
I love every time (...)

I love women. I love you. And envy you. And desire you. And *take* you. I love the taste of you. The feel of you. The sound of you. The thought of you. After three thousand women, I stopped counting... Now, you can believe this or not, what's it to me, but I have never chased a single woman in my entire life. The married ones neither, ha-ha-haaa! In that respect I am quite timid. Seriously. You're the ones who've always come running after me, oh yes you have! Even when I was a young boy in nursery school, in *maternelle*, the girls would fight over who got to sit next to me. Womanising was a way, I suppose, a subconscious way, to overcome my timidity. Cos I have never been disappointed; never once picked up the whiff of a woman who I thought wanted to, only to find out she didn't after all. Never. I am not callous, I swear. Think what you like. I am as I am. And I like myself that way. Besides, I now have a reputation to live up to. Some people think I'm stuck up, think I think I'm clever. Well, I *am*. I'm exceptional. I'll leave the rest of you to be ordinary.

We sat in the car and the talk came easily:
I love women. I dunno. You impress me. If you ask me, a woman is in her sexual prime between thirty-five and forty-five. That's the age I like my girlfriends to have although my current girlfriend, she's fifty. I've been screwing forty year olds for over twenty years now. Older women are still attractive. Sometimes. When they are well-kept. But it's not the same. Their skin... their tits... their behind, it's just not the same. When I was younger, the women I screwed were all a good ten or more years older n me. Some of them'd still like to go to bed with me today, but they're old grannies now, seventy and upwards. What do I wanna be screwing them for? We can go out for a drink, for a meal or a chat, but that's about it as far as I'm concerned. Sex is part of life and it's as natural as breathing. Don't ruin it with false morals or too much thinking. I need sex. I always will. Sex is like a good glass of wine. Nothing more. It's there to do you

good. Our bodies are there to do us good, and every single part of your anatomy serves this purpose. As long as I'm alive, I can't live without it. And as long as the young girls like me, what do I wanna be fucking a granny for, pardon my French!

Young girls like me cos I know how to make love. The young men no longer have the skill. They waste their time with stupid computer games and wot not. You want to know what I think? I think the vast majority of the world's population has never had a decent *fuck*. When you think about all the moral and religious cobwebs people have... look at yourself and you consider yourself enlightened or progressive! Like hell you are! You've got this intellectual, superior edge to you but I can tell from the look in your eye that all this hoity-toity crap is just there to cover the fact that you need a good shag, don't you? Why are you sitting in my car? Cos you're after my life story? I've had women who confess that their husbands have never, ever, managed to make them come, or older women whose husbands wouldn't go down on them cos they still belonged to the generation of men who didn't do those things them days. I've made thousands and *thousands* of women happy; woman who had never tried anal sex or the positions I initiated them into. Women who've never had such a bombastic orgasm that they come all over the place and think they're pissing. But they're not. Every woman is a *femme fontaine*. Few are the men who know that. Women who hate oral sex with their husbands because the disrespectful swine don't even bother to pay attention to their hygiene and smell like a toilet, such women suck me for hours and hours. They want me to come in their mouth, then stick my dick up their arse. I give them what they won't get anywhere else and that's why they come back for more.

44

I was in the disco, once and at one point in the evening, I got dancing with a lady who was fifty-eight, it transpired. We had a few drinks and a decent little flirt. Women talk more openly than men, so we soon got personal. She confessed to me that a man had never, *ever*, been able to bring her to an orgasm. Now, if you are a normal, healthy woman, the problem doesn't lie with you. I told her, OK, rendez-vous. Are you joking, she asked. Nope. So we met on the arranged date and I proved to her she was a normal, healthy woman... She came back. Again. And again. I even introduced her to my wife as an old friend. She was a woman of her word, and never told a soul. It's not your problem. It's ours. So many lousy fuckers out there just passing the parcel.

I love women and women feel loved by me. I respect them. No women is made to feel like a whore when she's with me, even the whores! I've been with whores, of course I have. But I don't treat them as such. I respect and love them as much as I love any woman and they appreciate it. Their orgasms are real with me and not faked. Imagine a hooker saying thanks to a client, ha-ha-haa! *(Helpless smile...)* I love women. Genuinely. *(Hardens...)* If you call me a chauvinist, you haven't understood a goddamn thing.

*

It cannot be right.
It can not.
To be attracted to this:
Man
Goddamn!
You say you have never chased a woman in your life,
But you know exactly why you say

The things you say
In the presence of a woman;
To her drowning eyes;
Goddamn!
Know what it will do to her insides...
It is poison.
It is bait.
So, of course, all you have to do now is sit back

and wait...

*

Welcome to my parlour said the spider to the fly... Any considerate lover will have a den: somewhere to take his lady to. It's tasteless to go to some cheap hotel, like a Formula 1, where you can't even clean yourself up properly afterwards. You go there, you wham-bam, and then you bugger off? It's like meat without the salt and pepper. No taste. No woman's going feel at ease with that, it'll make her feel like a whore, but you're not gonna lay five hundred on the table for a good hotel just for an hour of fun, are you? Anyway, it's not the same. You haven't got all the accoutrements; a good bottle of champagne, some nice music, somewhere cosy and familiar. And at the hotel, there's always that look of the receptionist. She knows exactly what's going on: Knows that one, or both of us, will be married, so that makes your lady friend feel even more like a whore. I don't give a shit what the receptionists think, but I like to show consideration for my damsel of the day. No, you need your den. Your little retreat.

If you want to keep a woman, you've got to put her under pressure. Don't let her know where you are all the time. Keep her guessing. Let her wonder: is he really out with his mates, or off with a lady somewhere? And if he is out with his mates, is he out with the ones he said and are they going where they said? If you don't spice things up, it'll soon turn tasteless... Who wants food that tastes of nothing? But she, and here's the beauty of it, she'll be so keen to prove that she is true, she'll be dropping you little messages all the time, letting you know where she is: darling, I'm just off to do the shopping. I'll be back at three... Nature's on the side of us men, innit?

I, Tatar, am faithful of the heart, if not of the body... She knows that, and She knows She cannot change me. None of you can change me. Do you think *you* can change me?
If She suspects something and asks me, I shall tell Her. Medicinal lies. She knows She cannot change me. It is my one weakness.

My current girlfriend? She's more than I ever hoped to find in a woman. She's kind. She's desperately in love with me. Every test I have put Her to, She's passed it. She hates smokers, yet She's even reached the point where She'll buy my cigarettes for me and light them up. I promised Her that I'd stop smoking. I'm trying to cut down, to lose some weight, too; get a few kilos below my normal weight so that the kilos I'll put on once I stop smoking will be accommodated.

She is the sweetest woman I know and I want Her to come and live with me. But I don't love Her. I like Her a lot, of course. And if I ever find out that She's two-timing me, I'll ditch Her. Never a bad word has passed between the two of us. Normally, my relationships work well for a short time, then we start tearing each other to bits. She is everything I have ever wanted. If it doesn't work out, I might as well turn over and die, for what else do we live for? When I come home late at night, She doesn't reproach me, She just massages my back for a good hour before going back to sleep...

A lovely woman. A sweet woman. *(Change of tone)* But She doesn't turn me on... I'm teaching Her how to pay more attention to Her appearance. It's not just because you're fifty that you no longer need to make an effort... The jeans I bought Her, She didn't want at first. They're the sort of jeans my daughters wear, She protested. Anyhow, I bought them. And guess what She puts on more than anything else, ha-ha-haaa! A man wants to be proud of the woman by his side. People can't look into her head and see if she's kind or a bitch, if she's intelligent or simple. They can only see what's on the outside. You have to take care of your appearance. My mother taught us as young boys: if you're wearing a red shirt, wear red socks. If you're wearing black shoes, put on a black belt to go with it. It doesn't take much, see, but you have to develop an eye.

My previous wife had a great sense of fashion. But she cost me a fortune! This one'll never compare, but She can still make an effort. She was married for twenty years to some jerk who never managed to satisfy Her in all that time. She must think She's in heaven now. *(Change of tone, puzzled...)* Somehow, I dunno, I can't ejaculate with Her. I fake my passion and She can't tell the difference cos I always manage to satisfy Her. Every time. But because She doesn't do it for me, I'll always have someone else. I said I would never live with another woman cos they're all too complicated and things always turn sour in the end. I have been married three times; I

know what I'm talking about. I want a woman? I have a phonebook full of women. I can have a dozen different women a day if I wanted to. Women come. Women go.
- And despite everything, Tatar, you yearn for one who will stay...

You can't change anything in this world, so why try? We are so insignificant. You realise this when you're dead. The world goes on without you, not taking the slightest bit of notice of the fact that you were once there. No matter how mighty you are, even if your fame lives on for thousands of years after your decease, the world continues and you can't change a goddamn thing. When you sleep, you're dead, too. You can't do anything, can't change anything. For years, I never had more than five hours' sleep, because I had no time to waste. What a fool! What a bloody waste of time, ha-ha-haaa!

I am God. Don't look at me like that! God is man. Every single one of us is God. If I were God, I would do things exactly as he did, concerning us humans. I would make a man and a woman. Like him, I would make the man strong. And stupid. And the woman weak. But intelligent.
Yeah yeah! If it were the other way round, strong intelligent women and weak stupid men, we'd have no chance of survival. You'd have us on a leash and lead us around like a pack of hounds. The way things stand, we have the force to keep you in your place,

ha-ha-ha.

Haaa-ha-ha!

Normality? Normality? What's that when it's at home, if I may ask? Normality is always presumed to be somewhere else. But take a good look around you. No-one is normal. There is no such thing. No-one is normal. We are all perverse. Every family is a putrefying slop of violence and beastliness in subtle, or less so, forms.

How can it be otherwise, when families are made up of individuals like us?

I said individuals like *us*, not individuals like me...

How can our societies be otherwise, when they are made up of families like ours?

I said families like *ours*, not families like mine...

How can the world be otherwise, being home to the societies we breed?

I said the societies we *breed*, not the societies we need...

Normality is elsewhere, and you know what?

Not a fucking soul lives there.

*

Carmina, after her marriage had broken up, allowed herself one day of mourning. One day. For her. Not for him; to tell him all the things she had wanted to say but which acrimony had left no room for – the love, the regrets, the growth, her own way, away from him, which he could never understand and which he therefore, finally, classed as malicious egoism. Men don't respect women they can have. Whilst they are still courting you, okay, but once you are theirs, respect is soon usurped by critique. Suddenly, or gradually, that marvellous woman is no longer good enough. This must change, that must change. The changes came. Oh yes they did... She ran the film of their co-existence, like you do as the white light pulls you with its forceps from death along the passage to a new life. She walked, fearlessly, to the light and upon reaching it, turned around, only, briefly, to press his eyelids down, gently, with her thumbs.

You come alone.

You go alone.

If you are blessed, you may sojourn a while with other souls, but they are not yours and you are not theirs. Refusal to bow to this does not alter the facts; it will simply rob you of your serenity; of the ability the see every day together as counted, and blessed.

Catch the day to day

Live the day

Today...

Carmina walked through the well-tended courtyard, where the blades of clipped grass conspired to suck the truth from her faltering steps and shushed the secret from the one to the other, bowing low as they did so.

Shhhhh. Shhhhh...

She rang the bell, ensconced in the wall like a raisin forgotten in the hardened dough. Clutched her gift of flowers to her chest, shading an inexplicable guilt...

Roses = the petals of bleached pink curled dirty around each other, pressing the secret of their beauty deep into the elusive centre of their wafered complicity...

I like beautiful things, as you can see... I used to paint. In fact; I used to paint a lot. Under a different name. I have commissioned some paintings, but the artists have hardly ever really captured what I was after. They've never really understood me. Too many nerds gallivanting around out their calling themselves artists, but what sort of an artists are you if you don't have this sensitivity? I bought the paintings anyway. I am the decent type. Take this beauty: what are you smiling at? Don't you like it?

Quite a while back now, I commissioned Charvet for a painting of a fat-arsed woman, and what I got back was: a fat-arsed woman,

but not the fat arse I wanted, you see.

Never mind. Anyway, it's no mere coincidence that this painting's hanging up the stairs on the way to my living room. It's the first thing you see before you enter the heart of my domain; a fat pink arse sitting on the barbed-wire fence of a meadow - looks like a meadow to me - the arse of some overweight wench with her dress up to her waste and her drawers down to her ankles, ready to drop a big turd, go for a piss, or maybe just let the stench of the air she is about to pass mingle with the sweet country breeze instead of being caught up in her underwear like a penny fallen through a hole in the lining. Clever, funny, in a sense, the mounds of her ruddy flesh perched on that delicate strip of barbed wire, pricking into her...

but it's still not the fat arse I wanted.

Going up the stairs to my living room, every guest meets this painting eye to eye. A real frontal, if you see what I mean. Normally, I don't even comment on it, I just stand back and take note. I like to watch how people react to being greeted by a fat arse; by having it shoved into their face. Some people say nothing at all and walk on by. Others are quite shocked, if they say so or not. You can see the conflict negotiated in their facial muscles, twitching like a fly dazed by the windowpane it has just crashed into. Treacherous transparency! Others find the fat arse quite amusing or ask me something about it. Whatever the reaction, I get an insight into my visitor and a feeling for how to deal with them in future; you *never* get a second chance to make a first impression.

Everything you see here is for sale. I made my money in the antique business. One of my many passions. I like paintings. I've got over three hundred paintings hanging up in this place. Ganda. Levatic. Cammissar. Zivny. Mann. Nemmgati. Hueber. Wenig. Kovacik. Koliha. Bocker. Maur. Novack. Sindelar. Tazler. Veselak. Charvet. Bernard. Herbet... For the right price you can walk off with anything that takes your fancy... That one's nice, isn't it? It's called The Temptation of St Antoine. Watch your head. This used to be an old barn. Some of the beams are low.

I spent over ten years in and out of museums and galleries. Three weeks in Paris every summer, soaking up culture. Especially with my second wife, Marianne. Hélène, my third wife, was a blockhead. I don't think she's ever read a book in her entire life. She thinks she's smart and chic, but a person's face'll always tell you if they're bright or not. And I don't care how much of an effort she goes to with her make-up and her hair-do, when I look at her now, all I see is a face that looks like a pair of worn knickers; all skidded and crumpled.

Take a look at this one. Have you ever seen a tackier, more peevish frame in your entire life? The picture's a masterpiece, as far as I'm concerned. But that frame, what an eyesore! At first I wanted to throw it away and get a decent frame, something ornate and gilded. And just as I was about to, I thought, hey no, don't do that! You can't do that. Keep the original frame for its documentary value. It gives you an insight into the materials these poor artists had at their disposal, their framing techniques, etc. You see that they framed their pictures with anything they could get their hands on. They couldn't afford to be choosy. You see what sort of glues they used, etc etc.

That one twist more, that one step further in the convexities of your imagination, and the ugly is ugly no more... Just goes to show; there is no truth, but that we make it. You can string half a dozen people in front of a painting, and each will come to a different truth. What is art? Who decides what is precious? Who is authorised to confer such an etiquette on an item; to brand the hide of the cow? There is no art. There is no science. There is only... imagination, desire, and the quest for inner equilibrium; the need, the willingness to construct that other world which is so much more beautiful, more reliable than the one we live in. What is truth? Truth is every single man... Anyhow, some first class Czech impressionistic paintings hanging in my bedroom. Show you later.

Maybe.

Not even the decency to blush; to look away – every single blade, inebriated by the generous hospitality of the shrill spring sunlight, propped itself up to watch her, brazenly, assessing the weight of her every step. Her feet fell, one, two, left, right, on the slabs that ate their way through the lawn. The thud of her heels sending corrugated messages out, like Morse code, which the lawn decrypted skilfully then passed discretely on:
(finger to mouth...) Ssshhhh! Ssssshhhh!
So that by the time Carmina reached the garden gate, the last rowdy blades of grass were at the ready, wrenching their necks, clambering over one another in anticipation.
Nodding suspicion.
Carmina. Tatar;

54

Ssshhhhh.

Sssssshhhhh... By the entrance to the courtyard stood a tree whose leaves, x-rayed by the sun, showed their bones, like the veins scarifying the inner thighs of a redhead. Like a gooseberry. Just as Carmina had many a time seen ducks do, the leaves preened themselves this way and that, their fastidious movements coughing up shadows onto the grass.

Shadow = the patience of a thought with complete faith in your courage to stretch your hand beyond the portal of your fear...

Ssssshhhhh?

*

Truth cometh before the man.

Truth is bigger than the mind of man.

Man-made truths are but an impoverished
Fingernail full of the substance:
Of the brick that makes the mighty wall.

We scratch.
We dip.
We do not fathom.
The magnitude eludes us,
Thus, we
Do not conquer.

The search for Truth,
The confrontations with our limitations,
Take us to the discovery of Divinity;

Put us
Back
In our place,
Amongst,
Not above,
The order of things.

For the 'truths' we know are but language;
No one may speak them all.
We learn the beauty of sound
So that we may marvel at the Mother of Silence.

      Carmina was not the type to pray. She sat in her car, outside his house, his shrine, beyond his view. She sat. She thought. Passers-by would peer in, wonder why her lips were moving, her brow furrowed; her thoughts pushing their way through like young life climbing out of the tender soil with so much effort, elbows and all, it made you wonder why nature could not have been more compassionate. To the passer-by, Carmina's body appeared as mute, as limp as a sodden dishcloth, flung over the steering wheel. She's just come out of that church across the square, thought some. She's getting herself geared up to go to confessions, thought another. She looks sad. She has just suffered a bereavement. She's talking herself in, or out, of something. I bet it's a childhood memory, a painful recollection that someone else has unwittingly aroused, and which she is trying to shush back to sleep; an infliction too deep to heal, so she buried it and said amen. If you ask me, she's had a few too many: I'd go home by train, if I were her...
Carmina's mind laboured; contracted, screamed, pushed, gasped, marvelled, till the sun went down.

I am a female gatherer.
I harvest the faith.
I feed the hungry as part of my trade.
Catch the day to day.
Live the day
Today...
Suck it to the marrow.
Compress it onto swollen eyes
So the puff sighs out
So the eyes may see.

Yes, I am a healer.
Of a kind.
A believer
In my faith
To uproot
To the jellied heart
Of transparency.

And now, it is time for me to dive.

Every woman who's in love with you wants to have your child. I always make sure my women're safe; are you taking the pill? D'you have a coil? I never come inside them, even if they try to get me to. Out of all these thousands of women, I only have a doubt about possibly making two of them pregnant. Even here, I'm not sure. I would need to do all the tests imaginable to be one hundred per cent sure it was my child, but then, once it was clear, I wouldn't leave my child in the lurch. I'm very faithful, as I keep telling you. I talk too much, don't I?

Having children's the beginning of the end of the life of a couple... As a man, you take the back seat from then on. As long as you know this, it's alright, I suppose... Having children massacres a woman's body... that's another cause for the beginning of the end. Childbirth pulls a woman all out of shape and leaves a gaping hole that nobody ever talks about. Muscular re-education classes: what a load of crap! Did your midwife say to you: after childbirth, your tight little pussy's gonna turn into the bloody tunnel and when he's up there, he won't feel a thing? Has any woman ever admitted to you that her fanny feels different after childbirth? Yeah, yeah, it supposedly creaks back into place like an old church door... You can feel the contractions of it, and then everything's hunky-dory. Bullshit. Bull. Shit. You're the diver: air the secret.

A friend of mine paid huge amounts to a doctor to make sure his wife delivered by Caesarian... A woman only tightens up again when she's pregnant once more. Her pussy gets nice and tight and it's great for a man to be in there. I don't know why so many women feel it's wrong to have sex when you're pregnant. It's great! I've treated myself to a couple of pregnant women. Marvellous! I got onto the womanising track when my first wife fell pregnant and didn't want me to touch her anymore. Her loss, not mine. Plenty more fish in the sea, *n'est-ce pas?* But then the child gets born, and it's flappity flap all over again... You see those young mums with their great figures; their narrow hips and their perky backsides. All well and good, but if they birthed naturally, I don't give a toss how narrow their hips are, there's a whacking great hole in the middle. And those girls, children, you almost have to say; thirteen, fourteen, fifteen, sixteen, who're already mums, what a shame.

You can write them off for life... Why do you think husbands drift towards anal sex? Cos they want to *feel* something! The problem with anal sex, though, is that the women take a liking to it, then don't want it any other way. Yeah, and why do they take a liking to it, hey, hey? I go the anal way with women who've had their children naturally, cos some of them have a fanny that's so loose, you can fit your whole hand inside. Two even. Same goes for some backsides, sorry to say. A woman's arse is looser than a man's cos she hasn't got the prostrate gland taking up some of the space. My poor little dick's been worked so hard in his life, it's become insensitive. If I'm gonna wank, I have to give it a real good yank. And if I'm in you up front and can't feel a thing, then I'll turn you round... I refuse to wear a condom. I belong to the old school. Condoms don't protect you from anything. Do you put a condom on before she gives you head? Do you put a condom on your tongue before you lick her out? Or when you kiss? Ever heard of a finger condom? Ha-ha-haaa! You just have to choose your partners carefully. Men only have a four per cent chance, women an eighty percent chance of catching something if you sleep with a contaminated partner. I do a blood test every six months. And I steer clear of junkies.

I don't know why so many men're afraid of a woman's fanny, or find it dirty. Truth is, it's the cleanest space in the body, I read somewhere. Yeah, it's got germs, but they're there for a purpose. They've got a job to do. In a healthy woman, these germs're the same as to be found in yoghurt. No kidding! They're the same lactobacilli. And one of the things that can make this yoghurt turn sour is us, I mean, male sperm. A healthy vagina is supposed to be acidy (between pH 3.8 to 4.5, to be precise). That compares to a glass of red wine. And oh, I do love my wine, ha-ha-haaa! Semen is alkaline; pH 8, or thereabouts. It's the most alkaline of all our body fluids, and sometimes, the vagina has problems getting her balance back after a shot of this alkaline brew. Works best, apparently, when the vagina recognises the sperm as being that of the woman's regular lover. See, nature's put a spoke in your wheel when it comes to screwing around, too, ha-ha-haaa! And the moral of the story is: ...

If you ask me, most men don't really love women, as I do. They're afraid of I don't know what; of getting their dicks bitten off, of being in that dark, moist cave they cannot see, they're afraid to taste you... to do the things you need to feel sublime. I'll do anything you want; I'll do you both ways, from the front, from behind, I'll lick you, eat you, even if you're menstruating, cos I know, that's when you like it most. I'll do anything, anything, to please you, because I love you, all...

I think most guys, let's say eighty per cent, are gay. They don't really like women at all, most men. You know, the real odour of a woman. They prefer to slap each other on the arse, call it sportsman's behaviour, and peek at each other in the shower but they'll never admit to the fact that it turns them on. I reckon that there're very few men who really love women. Like me. And that's why there are so many of you whose bodies are secretly weeping. Like you.

*

It cannot be right, it cannot -
Goddamn!
It is poison
It is bait...

And if -
Small word with big implications...

*

Time,
It's not something we have
It is something we take.
Not something that's there,
But something we make,
Like Verity,
Honour,
Science, like Art...
Like the lover we create
From the rib of a simple man,
Lodged in the longing of our heart...

Time;
To reflect
Retrospect
Project
Reject
Renew
Re-tell
Re-live
Forgive
Forsake
Forget
Fornicate...
Celebrate
Re-conciliate,
Masticate
Digest...

Time
To string a rosary
Of faded bliss
I may finger
At my behest
And pray

Time
To clear out
That mess in my head
I call them my thoughts
But what's the use, anyway...

Time,
To bury the hatchet
Between mother and child
Between husband and wife
Between State and People
Between Faith and the Steeple
Between body and mind
Between what I may keep
What
Leave behind...

Between the hungry, the satiated
Between the classes
Between the races
The places
Carved up and dished out; That's yours
That's mine
As we do with our time...

Dismembered
Like my faith

Like my aborted love
Like gutted pride...

Distended like my sighs
As I comb the horizon
Knowing that what I seek
I shall never find...

Joy Stick

Hold it in your hands
strike it softly
suck
till your thirst of semen
is satisfied…

Kiss it all around
the warm, vibrating
tool of your desire…

Let it softly come into you
and then push, push, slowly…

Get it down.

Get it done.

Neighbour

From her window, her face chequered
by her curtains
she had a
direct view of her neighbour
about 60m away:
of neighbour's son.

Even from that distance one could tell he was
strong;
that there was muscle
under his fat...

They owned two large tractors they would manoeuvre
in -
and out of their
tight
courtyard
early in the morn and late in the evening; that took skill...

He was bald; by choice
Skin...
Head...
Made you notice his
neck; his big shoulders...
working in the field all day
that's bound to make you strong...
the way he walked, too...

From where she sat everything about him said:
Man...
Strong...

And she had noticed that the only female in the house
belonged to his father

So, big, strong... lonely man...

When she drove past in her car as he
mounted
one of those virile metal beasts she tried
not to look but at the last minute
she couldn't help it: she looked up -
and he:
smiled down...

Clean white teeth

Skin...
Head...

He waved
she waved
safe behind her windscreen.

Only an old woman in the house
two men
and a Dobermann...

He was not from here she had heard...

Seemed not to have any friends

Quiet?

Mmm, and discreet...

Tramp

I want to feel your nose in my lips
your nails in my flesh
your teeth on my hips
your breath in my face
your tongue -
wherever it fits...

I want to feel your dick in my ass
you come in my throat
you spit on my skin
your balls beat me raw...
your hand pin me down

and Master me

Freak? Me?

I want to hear you moan
groan
whimper
I want to see pain on your face
delight
abandon
release...

Rough me
ride me to a froth
burn me
whip me with your Man till
I spit blood

And I?

Will bathe you with the purity
of my softest womanhood
till I
oil you
rim
purring with gratitude…

But first, you polish me
if you want to see my genie

If you want to see me shine.

Genderlogue

Mother's mother's ruminations on the modulations of love:

You cannot love a man for all your life. But you *can* live
with him. You can live with him whilst you love him,
though sooner or later, that love will fade to irritation and
putrefy to hate. The art therein is to wait. Wait... Till hate
has healed to indifference, then you will find him liveable
once more,
beyond love,
beyond hate's horizon;
from the better,
to the worse, to the:
oh well, I guess that'll just have to do.
For it will, you know. Do.
Self-preservation will stop you from hating him all your life.
Why put the shamrock to your lips like that?
No, save yourself the strife.
If courage, or necessity, makes you take your vows
seriously, you'll have to stop hating or else you'll start
berating yourself.

How courageous are you, daughter of mine?
How needy?
Or greedy?
How steady, or ready to go it alone,
if you believe yourself to have
outgrown the love that made you bloom
before it made you wither?
You dive, I know.
Deep, deep you want, and claim to go.
Though this be brave,
are you equally prepared to ride the wave -
to be soused but not drown,

have the strength to stick around.
For Verity?

Times change,
oh, haven't I lived long enough to see that!
Moods change. Morals, too.
All these fabricated things will pass, yet truths
are more enduring.
A man should never be your reason to be,
so let him be; let him stay around, on the periphery.
For Verity.
If you know who you are, what you want,
you know, you need not go under.
This ring on my finger? Take a good look.
Been there for centuries.
It's on my finger, right?
Not in my mind, for there's more n one way to read that
book...

I am who I want to be, even when life was unkind to me.
Haven't been in love for over sixty years and am sick to
death of hearing about this love fallacy. What you need is
something liveable. Durable. I'm not so much of a diver.
Call me a surfer. In any case, no less happy.

Daughter of mine, your skin is still so smooth, not
splattered with mildew like mine. You have so much
time...
so much...
your hands...
your pretty, dainty hands.
Where's your ring?
Oh, that's right, you have never wanted one. Your mother
took hers off, too, after all those years, tho the bloody

thing refused to budge and after grease and spit and nothing else would do, I had to get an old pair of pliers to cut the thing in two. You have never wanted one, have you?

Oh, daughter's daughter,
darling,
you think you don't need him.
Maybe not, only you can tell.
Cover my desiccated hands with your freshness.
Yes....

But you know, men?
They'll always be around,
That's the problem,

so might as well learn to live wiv em.

Letters to No Man

I Walked On By

It was nothing special. No-one noticed her. No-one saw me. I walked on by.
As always.

We walked past one another. Not as you and I do, but as she and I do. She walked with her head hung low; in another world. Dreamy. Far away. Far away for the others, but not for me.

I walked on by.
As always.

She knew me. I knew her. We had seen each other often enough. Never a word had we exchanged.
Only glances.

I walked on by.
As always.

Her face was framed by her long, shiny hair. Brown were her eyes, clear, shiny and large. Her lips, thin and well-formed. Her face was like any other, but not for me. For me, it was *my* face.

I walked on by.
As always.

She came towards me. Nothing special. No-one noticed her. No-one saw me. Just as always. The cars drove by. Blind, we were, to the people all around. She looked up. Clear and shiny were her eyes. Beautiful, her face. We looked at each other; a moment, a second, maybe. Not more. Long enough for a smile.

I walked on by. As always.

(O. S., 23. November)

Pleasure (25. November)

Good evening, Océane,

I hope you had a pleasant evening with your glass of wine and candlelight. I delight in candlelight. Wine is also fine.

To drink wine on one's own has something sad to it. It should be a convivial moment between people who like one another. The one tells tales whilst the other fills the glass. You drink to each other's health. Fill the glasses once more... Later in the evening, the empty bottle remains, a sign of the bond between the two of you. And a silent witness.

Have you ever taken a bottle by the neck and then, really, with your eyes closed, and with all the consciousness you can muster, discovered the bottle with your fingers? Felt, how the narrow form yields to become more generous... hard... round... Have you ever then buried your fingers in that hole at the base of the bottle to then circle its surface as though spooning cream out of a cup? I love to imagine how it feels to touch things. I love to touch things for real; to discover an object as though I were touching it for the very first time. This belongs to those many things we lose knowledge of as children, or rather, which we, as children, have driven out of us. Extirpated. Early in our youngest years, we hear: don't touch that! Yet to touch constitutes a primary form of encounter – we *grasp* long before we are able to understand. For all that words may be my trade, I like to let my other senses have their say, each speaking their own language. If, then, I take a bottle, I see its form, its colour. I hear the cork: pop! The glug-glug-glug of the wine as it is poured out; the music of it. I smell it before my taste buds have their fill. I hold the glass, allow it to sit in my hand like a pearl, or maybe I hold the glass at the bottom by its neck, like a pen, and let my little finger sway; conceited, but uninvited all the same. And then, I part my lips, stretched, full of anticipation, towards that glass...

My openness pleases you? Which pleases me! It is not to everyone's liking, you see. I'm labelled 'too intensive', and my art, it seems, too demanding. Children like me, as a general rule. I have a fine feeling for whom I may show myself to and whom not, which is also why I like to write. I need this honesty, this shamelessness (in its positive connotations). If no one else can bear it, then a patient sheet of paper that always will. I trust in the look we exchanged on that Saturday afternoon, for it was warm and inviting. I turned around, again and again, in search of this look. I found it. Its offer stood. I knew I would have to address you before I left; knew that you would be significant for me. In your eyes, I spotted the lad, that something playful, something cheeky. Your eyes were smiling at me, so I sent forth my child that she may play with yours. It does them both good, does it not?

In the cool of the morning breeze
My skin longs for the warmth of your love

Bared and shy she stands;
A child before your child -
Timid, though filled with the hope
That the two of you can play -
Want to play -
Shall play

Away all day -
Again and again till the

Sun-kissed breeze must
Cool once more
For the night moves nigh with the
Lull
Of her call;
Away, away -
Lie down my kin:
New games begin...

The Wind

He does not come. He is there. Wild, mild, impetuous. Passionate.

He shows me the meaning of spring and winter. Allows summer, allows winter to feel me. Darkens the days, brightens the nights. Gives me warmth. Passes me chilly flights.

My friend, the wind; plays, sings, laughs and whistles. A cheeky lad. Aiming a ball at the windowpane. Playing with the trees the 'catch me' game.

My friend, the wind; ruffling, tenderly, through my hair. Blowing me forth. Releasing me from the past, and showing me where the morning starts.

My friend, the wind:
Scruffy like hippies
Dozy like tramps
Ringing like bells
Burning like candles
Weeping like children
Wrecking like wars.

(O. S., 25. November)

Virgin (25. November)

Dear Océane,

Yes, I am already awake, have shovelled away the snow and had a cup of tea.

I'm wearing two pairs of leggings, my knee-warmers, my ski underwear (never been skiing in my life), a top which will not stick to my skin when I sweat. Gloves. A baseball cap. This will be my first snow-jog. I wonder which impressions I shall collect this time round. Each time I enter the forest, it rewards me with a new encounter. The play of colours, new every time. I have a notebook on me and stop, briefly, to swiftly write down the secrets the forest whispers to my ears. I am a collector, whose basket is never empty when I return home.

The forest will be quiet. Untouched, the snow...

In the early days, when my trips into the forest were merely occasional, I would always ask myself who these strange people might be; mad enough, whatever the weather, to run around in the forest till their faces lit up like a bulb. I myself started to jog one summer's day, on a day when I would otherwise most certainly have gone mad. The atmosphere in this house was unbearable and I thought: if I do not leave this house *on the spot*, somebody here will die... I got dressed and fled, literally, into the forest. I felt better upon my return. I went again. And again. The flight became a call. The forest began to speak to me. It listened as I laid my thoughts at its feet. Three months on, and I can no longer deprive myself of these encounters. Now, I, too, have become one of them;

the Wood People. My hour and a half will often pass without my seeing another soul. Other times, I literally run into fellow Wood People. Our eyes greet; we belong together. The same man, out for a walk with his dog, I see him every time. The people I meet depends on the time of day. The forest has its own rhythm. I even keep a lookout for specific trees, in the meantime, and witness their daily change of clothes. Whenever I am in the City, I am startled by the masses of people as they putrefy over the pavement. In such moments I long for home; I look at that flood of faces and think to myself, back home, each of you would be a tree, which, to look at, would bring me joy...

Goodness. Already 8 o'clock. I wanted to set off for my jog half an hour ago. Océane, I shall take you with me into the forest today. Wrap yourself up warmly.

All my love,

The City

A stone
Next to another.
A window
Next to another.
A door
Next to another.
A room
Next to another.
A brick
Next to another.
A chimney
Next to another.
A lock
Next to another.

One person
Next to the other.

In the City.

(O. S., 25. November)

The Better You (25. November)

Did You know that *You* could feel so;
Confiding, full of respect, of play...
Did You know of its many colours
Shaken from its sleeve in every way
To souse us with sunshine?
This, I did not know...

You are so close

you[1], strangely, not...

Therein lies, perhaps, that erotic touch; in this room that we, You and I, furnish with the thoughts we present to each other.

There is a crackle in the air...

A pleasure to Man

And Woman alike...

*

You...

---

[1] A distinction is being made here, based on the original German text, which contrasts the formal form of You (in German, Sie) with the informal form (in German Du). To capture this in English, the upper and lower cases are employed for *you* in the formal and informal forms respectively in the opening poem. Océane is addressed in the formal form throughout the correspondence until the last letter. For synoptic clarity however, the upper case is not used systematically in the English translation.

I know why this formal You pleases me so. It rewards our ears with the joy of a few syllables more: *give me... do You like it... show me...*[2] It is more generous to the ear, the skin and the mouth, for although it is as monosyllabic as the informal *you*, the former is more tender; caressing you by its very nature. The tongue vibrates in the cavity of the mouth, close to the teeth, though the two do not touch, so: *Sie*. *Du*, on the other hand, impacts; the tongue is pressed up hard against the teeth as the air is shot between both teeth and lips. Hence, *Du* makes contact whereas *Sie* merely hints at such. It is full of promise, creating room for development, for eventualities or future proximity. That, if you ask me, is the essence of the erotic; it is the space accorded to one's own fantasy. Suggestion rather than supposition. The wish to find oneself at some point in the future so that one knows how it went in the end...

---

[2] The distinction doesn't come across in English. In German, the text reads: *geben Sie mir... gefällt es Ihnen... Zeigen Sie mir.* Compare to the informal form: *Gib mir... gefällt es dir... Zeig mir...*

Trailing (26. November)

Hello Océane,

I have been sitting here for a little while now, yet am at a loss as to where to start. You say I want to say too much at a time. It is true, there is so much that I would like to share with you. I realise that I would like to please you and that your thoughts touch me. The best thing to do is for me to take my time with you.

The letters you read, as you now know, are not written with the same speed as your own. I stretch the time out so that my pleasure may be extended. Indeed...

One of your sentences I find myself reading time and time again. You say you are afraid of feelings. Of *whose* feelings, may I ask?

There was so much I wanted to say, yet I am surprised to see how my eyes now would rather look at my feet than hold your gaze. My timidity is not insistent. Don't worry. Soon, she will leave. Till then, I shall send you all I had wished to say, so: via my smile, my inclination for you and with the trust that you are able to catch.

Best wishes,

Time

Incessantly
It passes.
Melts,
As snow in sunshine.

Inexorably
It thinks.
Playful,
Like winds with our thoughts.

Untiringly
It breaks.
Destroys,
Like people do people.

Indefatigable.
Till nothing else remains.

(O. S., 26. November)

Between the Lines and Via the Heart (27. November)

Dear Océane,

If you had not already given me permission to do so, I would have to apologise for not being able to desist... You belong to me -
you early hours.

With the children still fast asleep, I sit here drinking hot water on an empty stomach (good for you), and indulge. I just have to pick you up again on what you wrote about the nature of our friendship. For two people to really get to know each other, you believe, words do not suffice. Not really. Tell me then, do you believe that you now know me better simply because we have spoken to each other on the phone? Can you appreciate someone more via their voice than by the written word? In a sense you are right, I suppose, because the voice brings you closer to a person's emotional state; it gives you the chance to see this person *live*, so to speak. Unedited. Having said that, what about those people who need time to show their feelings, and who manage this best in the written form, without necessarily aiming to convey an artificial image of themselves? Which means would provide you with the fairer impression of such a person; the trembling, timid spoken word, or rather the written one ? I suppose the biggest disadvantage of letter-writing is, of course, the in-built interactional delay, but isn't it precisely this which we both find so exciting? The wait... the reward...

There is a crackle in the air...

Do you travel a lot? Have you always lived in these parts? For a long time, I used to feel that I had no roots. Long story. We have time. In the meantime I regard the fact that I do not indubitably belong to a particular place as a strength rather than a weakness, for this grants me the freedom to wander where I will, both physically and psychologically. I realise more and more that where you see or deem your weakness might precisely be the place where your strength awaits discovery. My past was always a thorn in my side. You have to pay attention to where a person is coming from (geographically, psychologically) in order to better understand, 'see' where this person is now; to see what they bring, and what they've had to bear. The supposed burden of my past I now recognise to be my gift, for it has made me the person I am today; a sensitive woman, one who can delve, a woman who, for all manner of reasons, no longer regards herself as impure, but, on the contrary, as fresh, as new. I can laugh, I can mourn, I can forgive, wonder, and love. And I *am* in love... with myself. With Life. Life doesn't punish us, it rewards. It *is* a reward, and with this frame of mind, I drink to the last drop every second of my life, every gesture, every word and say

Thank you.

I run through the forest and say over and over again: Thank you. Thank you that I have finally cottoned on to what it's all about. I read your letters and say, Thank you! Thank you for your gift, for your warmth, which I take immense pleasure in and which I find inspiring. I give thanks for the little things as much as for the big things, then again, what's that supposed to mean: little, big? According to whose yardstick? I am happy, quite simply happy to be alive, to be rewarded by Life, and I would like to give something back, in my own way...

Océane, have you lit a candle already? I am just about to, and shall think of you as I do.

I take you in my arms.

All my love,

Gifts

The sun as it shines
through my window
on a morning.

A handshake, a touch.

A smile, a glance, a word.

A gesture. A letter. A call.

A picture, a book.

A flower.

A Thank You.

(O. S., 27. November)

Re: Candlelight (27. November)

Dear Océane,

Hello. I delight in candlelight...

No, I do not count the time I spend writing to you, nor do you hold me back from anything at all. On the contrary, and you know it.

What will tomorrow be like? I know no more than you do. Have no fear, for we have time. There will be many Mondays. Certainly, it will be of a different character to our letter-writing, the means being another. We shall leave the virtual world in order to enter the real one; akin to a birth in a way.

I like to listen when I am spoken to; listen quite precisely with my eyes as much as with my ears. I am looking forward to your eyes. Your lively, brown eyes.

Have no fear.

All my love,

Second Glance (28. November)

I would like to watch you as you write; the way you hold your head. How you sit, how you hold your pen and how your other hand is occupied. I would like to watch, to see if your face reveals anything of those thoughts you confide to paper with your voluptuous handwriting. What might your eyebrows be doing... what, that mouth, your fastidious, pleasure-loving mouth...

I grow afraid. I shiver. Were we too hasty in all of this? I don't want to lose you, for there is still so much, so much -

The best bet is to remain professional. Yes. Keep the talk to your professional projects. Find out which other projects this Mme Simonnet has in line. Mme Simonnet. Océane Simonnet. Océane... Don't let it show how much she ruffles you, how much you long to touch her, to feel the warmth of her hand on your skin. Keep it professional. There will be many Mondays.

I am looking forward to your eyes. Beautiful brown eyes, I see them before me, closed as they listen to the poems I have written you. I see you in so many visions I do not dare to share with you.

Am I too hasty?

I shall see you:
this evening.

All my love,

Ten Fingers

Ten fingers we all should have. The odd person has lost one, or a few, or the entire hand through: complicated circumstances - which don't count.

As children we begin to count.

With the thumb, we begin. We suck it, suck so long till the day arrives when mustard is smeared and the pleasure of sucking leaves.

The finger that points, that threatens, that reprimands, that sobers up, hammers, that changes the world.

The middle finger; pointless, meaningless. Suited for holding a fountain pen, but for nothing else.

A finger bearing a ring. Not every time. Cut off from its surroundings, as it were, extracted and even transferred, transplanted. A symbol of infidelity and oppression.

The little one, withered, scorned. We have our problems with this one. When we cut our fingernails. This one's the insects' darling: the first they sit on and sting.

And all of that as a twin pack. Mirrored.

Too little to do Good and destroy Bad.

Too much to do Bad and destroy Good.

(O. S., 28. November)

91

Postscript (28. November)

Océane,

If you really do write so much in such a short space of time – and that several times a day – then you must be quite a volcano! When's your birthday? How do you craft your letters? Don't you ever lose your line of thought? Do you want to know how I go about it? First of all, I read your letters

r-e-a-l... s-l-o-w.

I pour them over me and let them evaporate off my skin. I read them a second time. A third time. I take a piece of paper, a post-it or even an envelope, whatever's lying around within reach, and then I jot down some key words. Not one after the other, nice and neatly, as though I were writing a shopping list, just anywhere, wherever I happen to find the space.

Once I have actually started writing, a million other things suddenly occur to me, and they push and shove like pupils eager to board the bus on a frosty morning. Somehow, I find space for them on my slip of paper, too. One hour goes by. One and a half... even two, sometimes. The pushing and the shoving just won't die down, so I have to be firm and let the odd thought or two wait for a later bus, however loud they grumble.

I fly over my letter. Send it off. Hardly I have done so, then I think *stop!* There was something else I absolutely, absolutely wanted to say... That's how I write, most of the time.

And then there are those other times when what I want to say comes as spontaneously as a kiss: *do not fear...*

That's right.

I am a person who needs time and space. I take the time for you, and wish to grant our friendship space. It is not a bad thing at all that you are the reserved type. Pull me up by my lead whenever I get too eager. You have my permission to do so.

Best wishes,

The Armchair

We all have an armchair, a chair.
One's armchair.
One's chair.
It is there, somewhere.
Unnoticed, unsuspecting, misunderstood.
It's just there.
Waiting, maybe.
Day and night. Winter and summer.
Eyeing you, it is;
it knows what you feel,
what weighs you down,
what brings you joy,
what instils fear.
It sees all the coming and going.
Life and death.

Take a good look at your armchair. A good one.
You know nothing about it
and maybe you don't want to.
It knows you.
What you think.
It's there, listening along,
looking,
loving,
living along with you.

Take a look at your armchair, your chair.
Cradle, it is, to your thoughts.

(O. S., 29. November)

Adagio (29. November)

My dearest, dearest Océane,

　　Still you sleep, and justly so. I hardly slept at all, for to wake up could mean that I suddenly come to realise that none of it was true...
　　It was, was it not? Truly there? Not only in my fantasy, racing on? Yes, it was.
　　One word comes to mind: adagio. So beautifully, so slowly and with such devotion, you played my body. Phenomenal, for me, it was. I cannot, I decline, for the moment, to attempt to capture the magic of this evening in words. Rather, I shall let it remain such as it dwells in my memory. As music.

J.S. Bach. Partita No.2 in D minor (BW4 1004). Put it on. In it you and I shall meet once more.

All my love,

A Slither of a Touch

A minor gesture;
a minor, an unobtrusive gesture.

A glance;
a fleeting, an unsuspecting glance.

A word;
a teeny weeny, a vacant word.

A touch;
a slither of, a tender touch.

A kiss;
a brief –

an incredible experience.

(O. S., 29. November)

Blossoms (29. November)

Dear Océane,

I was out and about all day and have only just got back home.

There are certain things whose value, whose magic we take if we articulate. You gave me much more than a mere slither of pleasure, as you know all too well. I wish to say no more regarding this, other than that that young girl who entered your car at 7pm returned home a princess.

There is so much I would like to say, but it is time for silence. Time to feel. Remember. Melt. I can feel you. See you; your face, your boyish regard which says to me; it's not my fault, I can't help it. Your hands...

The butterflies do no want to be caught. I grant them their right to play some more. I look up, to the dancing of their colourful wings, and I cry with joy. One alone I permit myself to keep. In my heart...

There is where you shall remain. Always.

Affectionately,

Thoughts to Myself

I.
I am alone, but not so alone as to be truly on my own.

Everything around me is watching me, sizing me up, examining, lying in wait for me. Spying on, controlling me. From every corner I am being chased and attacked. And yet the sense behind this all-surrounding Nonsense is a thing I cannot feel, cannot grasp, cannot comprehend, all around me. I live it, simply. Impotently.

The bother of it.

II.
It is a roof that caught me to plug the holes the rain is leaking in through. Though the holes I cannot find, somehow I still manage to get wet. The rain
drops
indefatigably, insistently, chafing, monotonous.

It turns into a current that washes me away, that sweeps me along in a battle more desperate than my own may ever be. Win, I shall not. Stay? Indeed. But this alone will not suffice. It will wash me away; sweep me, from behind, off my feet.

III.
When I bend low, my vertebrae are set into motion. One after the other. A zip you cannot open. A zip which is jammed, but which moves, nonetheless; expanding, tightening, relaxing.

And when I bend low, my head could fall off.

And if there were a slope,
My head would roll.
And if there were a river,
My head would swim.
And if there were an abyss,
My head would plunge.

My body, however, would still be there, and one vertebra after the other would set themselves into motion, constantly in motion, one after the other, like a zip, opening and closing, till my head shall have been found and placed where it had been before.

IV.
The head that falls, the vertebrae amounting to nothing more than a closed zip, these are the times that crowd, that envelope, that surround us.

If time did not exist, then nor would we. She runs and runs, relentlessly. Yesterday is not Today, and the Morrow is not the Day Before. Time does not go backwards, she simply drives us back.

If it were not for yesterday, there would be no today. If it were not for today, there would be no morrow. Yesterday is the morrow for today. Time robs us of the freedom to live.
To live
Timelessly:
Now, that is what I call liberty.

(O. S., 30. November)

Re: Sweet Dreams (30. November)

Dear Océane,

Pretty was the candlelight. Soft, probing, your hand as were your lips. Your tongue. True, I would have preferred different circumstances so that we could fully savour such intimacy. There will be many Mondays.

As I was out in the woods today (yes, I managed it despite my lack if sleep), two observations remained in the end. Two clues, if you like. Firstly, the green of the leaves, there, where I had grown accustomed to seeing the fiery tones of autumn. Now, there was green; as small the leaves, as tender as in spring. They have survived the autumn, and have no faith, it seems, in winter. How fascinating! Secondly, I became conscious of my footsteps, and saw therein a metaphor for Life. For us, too; the tender greenness... the notion of being under way.

I have read your lines over and over again. They touch me in such a way that everything I wanted to say becomes superfluous. You are right. We feel the same thing. I shall say no more on the matter other than: Thank you. Thank you for welcoming me into your life and for all the warmth you give me. Thank you for placing that tender plant I confer upon you in a sunny corner. We shall watch and wonder at how beautiful it will become with time.

I grow tired after all. Pretty was the candlelight, especially when mirrored in your eyes.

Good night. Sleep well.

Feast for the Senses (11. December)

I took the extra-long route today. Amazing visions occurred to me as the sun shone down. Above all, I live it all as colour, music and dance. As I ran, I could feel that bundled energy between my hips. Memories stirred to life, lifting me to ecstasy. I screamed with joy. I wept. I wallowed in the breast of nature, in the light, like a hedonist.

I am still filled with the smell of you; as strong, as thick as a liqueur...

One hour left before the day-to-day takes over. I shall go into the garden. Sweep up the leaves. Sing. Let myself fall and be filled with joy.

With you.

All my love,

The Red Mao Bible

I lay there,
right on the ground.
Beneath me,
nothing but grass and brown earth.

I lay there,
with a candle burning brightly in a glass
I have placed on my forehead.

I lay there and read my book;
a book which might be the red Mao bible.

Maybe.

I lay there with no-one around to disturb me.

No-one can disturb me when I,
a candle burning brightly in a glass,
when I,
with a book that,
perchance,
might be the red Mao bible,
when I thus lay down
on the green grass
and the earth's brown.

(O. S., 13. December)

Recognition (15. December)

I wept, I shivered myself to sleep. Never has anyone spoken to me this way before. Easy to confuse with the critique which has stalked me all my life: you are too much of this, too much of that, you're no good at this, no good at that, either...

But I love myself just as I am. What is Woman, anyway? How must we be, to really be She? Who has the right to prescribe? Who lays down the law? How is woman defined by Man? What does Woman have to say to that beyond contemptuous guffaws?

Who am I? Do I know?

Yours is not the critique that will rob me of my dignity; that attempts to yank it from my hold as though I have no right to claims. Yours is

Love:

Princess, I see you. All your beauty. All your shadows. You are a beauty that may grow if you so wish...

Never has anyone spoken to me this way before.

I weep

I shiver

With joy

To Be or Not to Be

Am I
As I am
I am not
I am not as I can be

Could be
That I am not
As I should be

Should I be
As I am
I will be
How I can

Can I be
How I am not
Stay I shall
What I should

(O. S., 15. December)

The Red Room

Familiar
I considered myself
with my many rooms
my chambers
and closets

For everyone I hold a key
thought I
till the day
you revealed to me
the key
to a door
whose existence
had escaped me.

Indescribably at ease
you slide
you turn
and enter...

A magnificent chamber
whose virginity
astounds both you and me

Lips hand-in-hand, as
timorously

We bathe in the
lush, the
plush
crimson walls
in the light

of complicity's opiated
pulp
of a glutinous sin
that is not
to be called such...

Our meeting point, our playroom
an exquisite discovery:
Pandora
slumbered
unwittingly though

Where do you go
why
quicken your step?
will you leave me here
alone?

Though drowned in the heat of red
I shall shiver
with cold
if you leave me
behind

Stay awhile...

Force me not
to live
with such deliciousness
blanched by dustsheets
my velvets untouched:
my chamber
Furnished yet
Uninhabited...

Woman

I am woman to the invitation:
to the scent
of your proposal
launching us
beyond
already given oaths.

I do not ask
what it might mean
and make no more
of discrepancies
than to respect
the evident conflict

Between the good

Between the man who
should say
'no'
yet wets me
effortlessly
with that
glance
certain that
I
am
woman...

Wicked, they say?
should I seek comfort
in hateful lies
to counter

cries
of Shame and Ugly?

I heed not

So come, wondrous pain -
a child I grant suck
whose brow
I kiss:
delicious sinful hot –
but would
not
have it
otherwise...

Souvenir

Today
on a day like many others
I had the impulse
the need to feel your presence.

I reach for my folder
press
my hand along the
surface of the page
shushing compassionately
reading me...
the pages of your mails feel different
to the pages of mine;
they set a ripple going through
my palm
a passionate
hoolahoop
circling my heart
lassooing my groin.

Don't ask me why
for I can't tell you how
but I am so glad
so *grate*
ful for these pages
that I have not *ef*
faced
unlike you
for you know for me Touch
has a power which
Vision does not:

I cling
like a mother to her slavery-born child
because every second counts
every split
second that I am allowed
to *be* with you...
and I know that my heart will be broken
know this as I feel your limbs stir within me
long before explicit manifestations
I know this from the very start
as that blue eye pinned me
to the spot
challenging
the purchase -
so I know
long before your first misgivings
but I let go of what I know
for I shall kiss the pain quiet with my faith
when the time comes...
we will be granted a specific time together
then each will be alone
on one's own
yet with a memory...

I remember the things you didn't say...
I remember a faint smile
your smile at my fishing your thoughts
back to me
up and out of the freshwater of your day-to-day

I remember your hands
as they flick your hair from your face
as they swish across canvas
or run along the voluptuous

hardness
of sculpture...

I cannot forget your fingers
playing the melody of your fantasies to me;
so close, so far, so
candidly…

And then there are your lips...
to say nothing of your eyes...

I remember how you
pull
a garment
up
over your head
and how my gaze
sails
over your torso
kissing your
neck, your
breasts, your
heart
how my nose
glides across your skin
breathing in
the perfume I shall keep
sealed
in a flacon
in my mind

I remember falling to my
knees
in front of you;

my ear on your navel...

Must I stop?
here?
now?
why?
how?

How, when I remember all of what
has *not*
been shared:

I remember what I feel;
what you say
I cannot
possibly
but do
for I am not
afraid to...

Ten Tries

#1.
-So tell me...
-What?
-Do you take it down?
-Don't you?

#2.
When my gran comes with this old time talk about how good we wimmin have it today and she can't understand why so many relationships split up cos hell, they had it real hard back then but they're still together. They had a long day's work and still had to come home and cook and clean and boil the shit out of nappies whereas today all we do is buy and throw away. We live in a throw away society, she bemoans, and we've thrown away an eye for what really counts. She says we're spoilt! I say gran, by all respect, if you've got the right to vote, had people fight for your right to vote and then you get it after all this time, fool for you if you don't use it. I say I can't imagine a slave staying on once (s)he has the right to be free, but she says the comparison ain't valid, a husband's not your master, and I've been spending too much time in the wrong company that much was plain to see. A husband's not your master, I say? Great, we agree that we're equals, then? I say, if he can fuck around, I can fuck around. What's good for the goose is good for the gander.

These here are modern times. And she says, you don't have to stoop as low as they do. You gots to keep your dignity. And watch your language! I say, where's the dignity in that, grandma? Well, she says, if you can't take it, his womanising, cos they can't help it, it's in their nature, then get out, but don't stoop as low as him; all those years of schoolin n still so stupid, child? Always make sure you can walk with your head held high. God gave you a brain and it's not between your legs and it's not just there to keep your ears in place, so use it. Who's he foolin around with, then, grandma, I ask. Is he foolin around with a sheep? Is he foolin around with a dog? If he's foolin around with another *woman*, then isn't it in our nature, too? If you're a whore, alright, she says, but I don't want no whores in my family. If God had wanted men and wimmin to be the same, He'd have made em the same. He didn't, so don't you think you can do better. They're one half and you're the other half. Make sure you're the better half and not no whore. I ain't no whore, grandma, I'm just a woman. A modern woman. I want to say, with *needs*, but I know better. A modern woman, are you, she snorts. Well, don't be. Be an intelligent one. And hold your heddup!

#3.
- *(Woman 1):* According to my mama, my granny always favoured her son. Boys are more loveable, she had the cheek to say. If she had anything to give, he would be sure to get the biggest half. If she was ever going to ask how anyone was, it was always Dukey. Dukey this Dukey that: Dukey nice n fat now? Dukey got a big house over there? My mum was the one who scraped the money together to go back a few times to look for her and all she

could ask about was Dukey. I'm sitting in her yard, my mama told me once, in her yard paying her a visit and the neighbours would say Howdi Miss Pearl, you daughter come all the way from Europe to visit you, and there would be admiration in their voices, but my granny, what would she say, Yes Miss Edie, Morning Maasa Riley, yes, and Dukey doing all right for himself too him going to come an visit me one day. And she never lay eyes on him again for as long as she live. The bastard got himself knived cos he was bred to believe he had the right to everything. Including someone else's woman. And my mama prayed not to have any sons cos she couldn't be sure not to make the same mistakes with their education. And God was good enough to listen. And you listen to me and you listen good. Any son of mine, any man who takes me on, he's gotta pull his weight, and, hey: r-e-s-p-e-c-t!

- *(Woman 2):* A-men! And my granny once told me about a woman who spoiled her son and he got into thieving and got caught and they hung him. Just before they hung him, his mama was there, all weeping, and he said to her, Come here, mama, I got something to tell you, come up close. And she comes up close with her ear to his mouth... and he bites off her ear. That's for not raising me right, he said and spat her ear out on the ground before they hung im.

- *(Woman 3):* That doesn't exactly belong here, does it?

- *(Woman 2):* Course it does! We breed dem to be the way they are, we breed em that way! You breed a swine, it'll snort, it won't bray...

- *(Woman 1):* How many times have you heard one open the fridge n say: where's the milk?

- *(Woman 2):* And the damned bottle's staring him right in the face! But if you don't watch yosself, you'll be foolish enough to get up and go get it for im...
(woman 1 and 2 slap hands, laughing)
- *(Woman 1):* How many know the names of their children's friends, or where they live...
- *(Woman 4):* Or the names of their children's friends' parents, for that matter...
- *(Woman 2):* When the next vaccination's due...
- *(Woman 3):* Or the doctor's name or number off by heart...
- *(Woman 4):* Or the teachers', or the number of the school...
- *(Woman 2):* Or when school holidays are coming up... and those are the 'responsible' ones; those are the fathers setting an example for the next generation.
- *(Woman 3):* Fair enough, but you can't tar everyone with the same brush, let's be fair...
- *(Woman 2):* All I'm saying is: swine... don't... bray.

#4.
-So, tell me...
-What now?
-Couldn't you just hate men, sometimes?
-Don't you already?
-I hate these wrinkles more, look at em. I'm getting older. Wattam I doing with my life...
-Don't worry about getting older, just make sure you're getting wiser as well. N those r not wrinkles, nope. They're life-lines. Life-signs...
-Gosh, that's the nicest thing anyone's said to me in ages! I love you!
-So you should.

#5.

-So, tell me…

-(*deep sigh*) Do I have to?

-Do you do, like, everything – like, you know, everything – you fantasise about, or are there some things you just don't dare to mention?

-Well, I sometimes have this dream of being taken by a whole gang of guys, you know, one guy everywhere; one in my mouth, one up front and one behind, and they change over all the time n ride me till I'm raw. Then there are a couple more doing kinky stuff like biting me or sucking my toes

-What?!!

-You never had your toes sucked? God, it's the biggest turn on, I mean, the biggest, so there are these five or six guys doing all these different things to me at the same time n it's just, hey...

-You ever tried it with a woman?

-(*categorical*) No.

#6.

I sometimes imagine tying a guy up and suspending him in a frame, you know, like a fly caught in a web? He's writhing all over the place cos it really turns him on to be at my mercy. Then I come on, all dressed up in leather n studs, you know, n I got a mask over my face. And a whip in one hand. I kinda tease him a little with this whip, slashing his chest, his back. His balls. He likes it when I bite him. Then a couple more ladies come on the scene. We kinda circle around him, like a pack of tigers. Purring. Cooing. He's got this massive erection and practically begging us to do something about it. One of us starts to suck him off, then she climbs onto him and fucks him, standing up, whilst we others circle around and slash him or lick him, scratch, bite, whatever... She climbs down and another one starts to suck him off before she fucks him. This time round, he comes, you can see him shuddering and moaning. She climbs up to his face so he can lick her out, and whilst he's doing this, she squeezes his sperm out, circling her hips to smear it all over his nose and lips. Another one of us gives him a hand massage so the rest of us can have our turn. We're sucking him and fucking him, he's licking one of us out, fingering another couple and there's another one of us working his ass n it's just pure carnal lust that wins control. We get more n more frenzied, start screaming and grunting like a pack of madwimmin, hair and limbs flying, you know. N he's screaming and grunting in pure ecstasy, n with all this noise and the stink of sex we miss the point where his screams have taken on a different quality n suddenly there's blood flying, blood on our faces n clumps of his flesh in our mouths you see pieces of his flesh being tossed over our shoulders and then he's not screaming anymore and all you can hear is our lascivious lapping of his blood like she-wolves at a midnight pool... yeah.

#7.
-Have you noticed how that beauty of a man mutates into some helpless infant as your relationship supposedly 'grows'? He can't find a thing anymore, tidy up no more, cook no more. I reckon he would probably want you to wipe his ass but he don't dare ask...
-Girlfriend!
-I had one even go as far as to say that he didn't have his mother's breast to himself cos his thirteen month older

118

sister was always hanging from the other one. And when he started sucking on mine, girlfriend, believe me, it was not with the pull of a man who wanted to do you. And believe me, I felt truly, truly sick. Abused.

-That's sick. But when I think about it, when I was breastfeeding, yeah, you're right, he wanted my breast, too. That *is* sick…

-That sure is.

-They are, but you only discover by degrees.

-Because we tell ourselves we need em, so we inject them with the force we need em to have.

-Trouble is…

-M-hm…

#8.

-What I would nonetheless like to know from you is this: has an old man's hard-on got wrinkles on it? I really ain't never seen one that old before, either…

-Did he ever go down on you? Doesn't really seem like it…

-But there was this business with the strawberry…

-Some say they will but then they don't. I had this one guy, took three years of persuasion before he braved my Dark Continent n when he did, girl, I swear, he did so holdin his breath…

-You got to teach them what's good for them, that's all. My guy seems to have learnt *that* lesson well… Wants to eat pussy all the time…

-Something about the idea scares them.

-Maybe it's the smell…

-Smell? Pussy is perfume, honey. I love that smell myself.

-Maybe it's the thought of periods and secretions, childbirth n all that that puts them off…

-Well, sis, he ain't eatin that peach? I ain't licking that lolly.

#9.
(Woman 1): You wanna hear my theory about Erectile Dysfunction?
(Woman 2): I'm listening…
(Woman 1): It's him saying No.
(Woman 3): Yes, but to what?
(Woman 1): Either to you as a person, or to women in general.
(Woman 4): Are you saying he's gay?
(Woman 1): Nope, I'm saying I reckon you're too much for him.
(Woman 2): But he's the one who keeps insisting!
(Woman 1): Because he wants to prove a point. He wants to prove he's man enough to master you, but it's not your body he's not man enough for. At the end of the day it's your m-i-n-d. Hell, anyone can *fuck*! You just have to feel good about yourself. Confident, know what I mean? Cos if you don't, you can't. And he can't feel confident about himself no more cos he's not worth the half of you, and he knows it. And the more he comes to realize this, the more his friend goes on strike. *En même temps*, you, my dear, are waking up to the beautiful, intelligent, powerful, celestial woman you are. You're tuning in. And this destabilizes all of them. He didn't have this problem when you first met him, did he, or was he Mr Soft from the start? Well then! Anyone can make love. And now you know why he can't.
(Woman 2): …
(Woman 1): And the more his friend goes on strike, the more he's got a point to prove.
(Woman 2): …

(Woman 5): We've all been there, girlfriend. Take it as a compliment.

(Snorts all round)

(Woman 6): You talking about Tilmann or Egon?

(Woman 1): Tilmann, Egon, what difference does it make? N you know what? I reckon Maurice will join their ranks, too. One day...

(Woman 7): That one's into anal sex too much for my liking...

(Woman 6): Are you saying he's gay?

(Woman 7): I'm just making an observation.

(Woman 2): Til and I were almost at the end of our foreplay once –

(Woman 3): He managed to get that far? Well, congratulations...

(Woman 2 continues, unoffended): ...when he pulled out this dildo from beneath his pillow. I thought, when did you buy that? But then again, why not? Only...

(Woman 1): Only what?

(Woman 2): He didn't use it to gratify me, but... to... to gratify himself...

(Woman 5): You saying –

(Woman 7): He shoved it up his own ass?

(Woman 2): ...

(Woman 6): And then?

(Woman 5 to herself): That sounds like a pretty loud *No* to me...

(Woman 2): And then he came, like, buckets, all over the place. Over my face, the sheets...

(Woman 5, shaking her head): ...

(Woman 6): And then?

(Woman 2): I went to the bathroom. And threw up.

(Woman 5, shaking her head): ....

(Woman 6): And then?

(Woman 2): I sat there for I-don't-know-how-long. And when I came out, he had gone.
(Woman 1): Did he take his 'utensil' with him?
(Woman 7): 'Where's my dildo, darling?'
(Woman 3): 'I put it in the laundry, dear…'
Peals of laughter. They pull Woman 2 to them. Shower her with kisses.
(Woman 5): Is he at least good-looking?
(Woman 2): Who?
(Woman 5): Mr Mystery Music Man.
(Woman 2): In a faintly obscene, Klaus Kinski sort of way, yes…
(Woman 7): Who's…?

(Together): Keep the faith. Your beauty, your dreams… accept. Forgive, that lie? Woman is not weak. No, we don't need you. Never will I let any of you lay your Shit at my door again. We (fighting, fighting…) may stretch - may break through the stone, like the seed, to become our destiny. Sing, without rancour, Flowers of God, that we may never forget. That we may soldier on. Sing about Life. Distilled, its secrets. Dispelled, the untruths, lest they muddy our vision of who we Are (who else, *but I…*); of our right to self love. For self love is the first, the hardest step. But one day you be running…

#10.
-So, tell me something…
-What?
-Do you, well, you know...
-What?
-Do you, do you sometimes feel afraid to say what you think cos you think you're the only one who thinks like

that, and, you know, you're afraid people might get the wrong impression, think you're weird, or sick, n judge you, you know? N then they don't keep it to themselves but spread it around n when you look at people you think you see this look in their eye n you think oh my god they know all about me so, you know, you feel stripped. You feel as though you're walking down a high street n you've got no knickers on n everybody's looking n you can't explain, you know, let them know it's all a mistake, like, on the one hand you're walking, but on the inside, you're paralysed by shame?

-You want to know something?

-What?

-It's normal. You're normal. And precious, okay?

Exhaust

His sexual drive is like a motor;
it runs in cycles
apparently impervious
to our relational
barometer

When he needs ´it´
he comes to me;
tries to win me:

To fill his tank

To empty his ashtray...

Storyteller

Storyteller
I, the book
in your pocket
cushioned
within the folds of your cloth
as I wish
to be
within the folds
of your skin...

For that moment alone I live
when you feel
for me
ease me
free
run fingers
along my spine
arched receptively

Open me –
wide
expose my innerst
my fragile wafers
to your pleased eye.

Quiver I quiver
in your breath
as your face
descends
close -
closer
as you select

that place
whence your magic
shall commence
as you lift me
mouthbound
as I nestle
pliantly
recumbent in your hand
as you open me...

Freed from your lips
a smile runs to me
with the whispered news:
he is ready!

Enfin,
at last
my moment is come
you lick a finger...
that moment has come
for your rod
warm
wet flesh
parts deftly
breezes my lips to penetrate
the folds of me

I shall shudder at your touch
erogenous;
as thumb and forefinger pin me -
before...
behind...
I whimper, mesmerized...

Storyteller
how well you read me

Please me:

Hold me
cover me
turn me over
lose your mind, your spirit
your tail
in me...

Hold me
cover me
turn me over

Flick...

Petal the secrets I spread before you
inhale me
unwrap the tale
I long to devour
carnivorously
succulently

For to lick is not enough...

Confetti my face
my puerile hands
smear
innocuously from
ear to ear
your paper dust
clowning

and joyous.

Splash your talent
generous

For to sprinkle is not enough...

Clothed in droplets
I cannot but shiver, thus
thick
must be my make-up...

Storyteller
make
believe:
souse me
unremittingly...

Breathless
tale told
fasten my seal
piously
cushion me
glimmering in the heat of slumber
to your fragrant folds

The scent
of my home.

Two Tongues

You cannot imagine what it is you give to me

you can't imagine what it means to me
to be able to be inside you;
to taste you...
you are the most fantastic woman I have ever
loved

I had almost lost faith in myself as a woman

maybe there is a Lord up there, after all...

darling, am I saved or damned, I don't know...

if I fall in love with you
I'm lost -
all my defences will be
down and I make myself
as vulnerable as a child

I want to be your mistress for as
long
as
possible...

I can't allow you to have this
might
over me
... but I don't want to
force anything

how will all this end?

and I'm afraid...

I don't even want to think about it...
come here, bébé;
let me kiss you…

Better than Telly

"Hello love, I'm home." He hung his jacket up on his peg in the hallway.

"Hello love, I'm in the sitting-room."

Monica sat in front of the television, smoking.

They kissed.

Those days at Beverly's had done Monica good. She had regained a sense of herself. Bev had let her keep the dress, the sandals and the lipstick. For memory's sake. Anyhow, Monica knew now that she still had it in her; knew that a man would indeed look at her twice, and not necessarily her face only, either. That gave her the strength for another round of her marriage with Jack. If both were to put a little effort in, what a difference that would make; she fixed her skirt and put her feet up as soon as she heard his key in the lock.

Him: Where're the kids?

Her: Your mum's got em for the evening.

Him: Why's at?

Inner voice: She's past her prime. She really has let herself go. Doesn't do anything with her hair anymore. Doesn't make herself up. She's put on loads of weight.

Her: Oh, she wanted to and they wanted to. Gives us the chance to 'ave a little time on our own once in a while...

But Jack was looking at what was on telly. *Crossroads* was just finishing.

Her: Someone lost ten quid in the cinema last night. Ten bloody quid!

Him: You're joking! Anyone find it?

Her (smirking): I bet... *(picks a piece of fluff from her skirt. Flicks it to the floor.)*

Normally she was the one who had to do the listening when Jack came home worn out, he'd say, and tell her who had been larking around, or which foremen were getting on his wick. Nina and Ben liked to tell their stuff themselves, had already told her off once for pinching their news, so it meant that she didn't have so much to share when he came home from work. So today, she baubled her bit of news in front of his eyes for as long as she could.

Her: I did... *(lets the words slip out as though they mean nothing.)*

Him (bolting up in his seat): You! You! You didn't... did you -

Her: What the bloody 'ell'd you've done?

Monica sat back and crossed her legs as though he really *was* making a lot of fuss about nothing, and watched a freckly-faced kid in yellow do silly things with his eyes cos he was so mad about Bird's™ custard.

Her: Course I bleedin' kept it! You hand it in, they only pocket it for themselves, anyway.

She sighed; all this talking was getting to be too much for her.

Him: Wooo! Monica! Ten quid! *(Reaching over to hug his wife)* You found ten bleedin' quid!

He still couldn't believe it.

Him: Give us a kiss!

Her (complying, tutting): You been real perky these last few days. Like the cat that's got the cream. Anyfing you're not telling me about?

She raised an eyebrow. But it was nice to have him hug her and kiss her spontaneously like that.

Him: Don't be so daft, who'd be foolish enough to want me?
Her: Well, thank you very much!
He got up and switched the telly over to BBC.
Him: Ten quid, I dunno...
Her: We got somefing nice for dinner; steak, chips and peas... Monica slid her feet down to the carpet and ran her fingers through her hair for something to do.
Her. N'after that I thought, well, I thought we might take a bath together n 'ave an early night...
Him: And the kids?
Her: Call your mum n tell 'er to keep em for the night...

Holding hands. So they missed the nature program in progress on the BBC, and didn't see the speeded-up version of them rather luscious-looking tropical orchids bursting from their buds and palpitating into glorious, technicoloured life.

Monica lay on her back, her hair still wet, waiting, her Jack still in the bathroom combing his hair. His mind on Emily. What would it be like, this Sunday? Would she turn up? Course she'd turn up! She'd come nicely dressed like she was the other day, with her hair all styled and her fingernails painted and they'd walk up and down and laugh with each other. He could put on that fancy tie Rich had brought him. And his new second-hand jacket, the one she hadn't taken any notice of that last time. Where should he take her? He couldn't be going anywhere where anyone might recognise him, if Monica got wind of this there'd be hell to pay. Take her over to West London, to one of them fancy pubs? Buy her a glass of wine? Something medium-dry, and a little expensive? Maybe they could go for a walk through Hyde

Park and he'd buy her an ice-cream, he knew what, he could take her to one of the London markets, that'd be nice. Loads of people brushing shoulders with each other, hunting for bargains. He might even splash out on a trip down the Thames, hey, he bet she hadn't done anything like that yet! He would get to take her by the elbow and lead her on board. I'll take a vodka and lime. And a glass of medium-dry for my lady friend, Jack grinned into the mirror. They might even go somewhere quiet and she might even let him put his hand up her skirt... no, Jack my boy, that'd spoil things. No point in rushing things, is there? A bird in the hand, and all that. Right? Yet the thought gave him an instant erection that propped itself up to meet his rather curious smile. Anyhow, Sunday was still two long days away... and there were other things he supposed he ought to get over and done with.

Right, Jack took a deep breath and stepped out of the bathroom. Time to face the wife.

"Well at long last!" Monica sighed, in her mauve négligé that stopped just before the knees, the one which she would only put on for special occasions like when she had to go to hospital. "I thought you'd escaped out the window and shinnied down the drainpipe!" She outed her cigarette.

"You can be really daft, you can!" he forced a laugh. What with all that food and that hot bath, all Jack really wanted was a good night's sleep but that was out of the question he guessed, wasn't it? And he had better jump to it, too, before his friend down there -

"Look what I got 'ere for you..."
He spread his legs in front of her. Closed his eyes and wished himself in some dark corner of Hyde Park with his fancy tie on...

Jack didn't always like it, but he seemed to want her to do it this time. Oh well, get on with it, girl, show a bit more interest, after all, it was her bright idea, wunnit? She found herself thinking of Beverly of all people. As if by magic, Monica wasn't Monica anymore, but Moni, in her black dress and gold sandals, sitting at the bar. Being driven back to Bev's place. She was Moni with that saucy smile as she watched him make himself comfy on the sofa and feel for his flies. Lipstick, Monica told herself as she dragged herself to the edge of the bed and pushed her hair out the way. It's just lipstick...

House of Dolls

A lifeless mass at first sight; wood, lace and pretty girl's colours, with an entry of deep red velvet. Ageless, and yet it had remained unscathed, though the men in the house had often wished to destroy it - jealous, impotent rage - whenever there had been strife with the woman of the house. Except the house was female property, and men were not to lay their hands on it.

A house in a house.
Wealth within wealth.
Secrets within secrets.
Fear within fear.

"Did you dream of the house of dolls?" Jane's mother asked as her thin, fragile fingers worked free the thick rope of red hair and proceeded to brush it.

"No, mother," Jane replied unable to conceal her annoyance. Always this tiresome question, and the strained chirpiness in her mother's voice; she would like to know what it was all about.

"I would so love for you to stay in this room. Right up until your wedding day," her mother sighed. The envious weight of hair silked through her fingers. Jane, so beautiful, so unaware, her quick hazel eyes seeing only what they chose to see, and not the glow of her incipient womanhood.

Lara was almost afraid to touch her. For over an hour she had lain in her bed practising her intonation; "Jane, may I brush your hair?"

"Lara, what is it you keep whispering to yourself like that?" her husband had asked her.

"Me? Whispering? What on earth do you mean?" she pulled on her dressing-gown from a chair at her side, and slid down onto the rug at her feet before the horrid idea had the chance to mature in his mind that he might like to make love to her.

"Your lips, I could hear them moving," he insisted.
His wife scoffed, "Indeed?" There was something about the quality of his voice that had never ceased to vex her. "So, you could hear my lips moving." She moved away. "As much as yours do when you're lusting after one of the maids in your sleep, I wonder?" She could see him in the mirror of her Edwardian dressing-table, and secretly willed all the four posts of the repressive bed to collapse in the middle and crush him. Lara opened her jewellry-box. After a slight hesitation, she decided upon a ring. "I'll just go and see if Jane's already awake."

"I'm not a baby anymore, mother."
Jane was sitting on her bed, critically examining a hair on her thigh when her mother's nervous hand faltered on the doorknob.

"Did I ever suggest anything of the kind? Let me brush your hair, Jane darling, it's so beautiful."
The child chatted on about school, about her house-mates, their hockey team, about the new riding-mistress. Margaret's father had bought a new Rolls Royce, and Hannah, whose father had been some insignificant colonialist in India who had made his fortune selling

precious stones - reputedly smuggled - well, Hannah was going to have to leave because they had run out of money.

"And she says she won't be the only one having to pack her bags, that we'll all be dropping off like flies. Mother, are we having financial difficulties, too?"

Mrs Castle-Gordon had announced that, due to insufficient donations, the building of the new stables would have to be postponed – indefinitely. All the girls, obediently gathered in the Assembly Hall, had thrown disappointed looks at one another and fidgeted with the hems of their skirts.

"Are we, mother?"

"I wouldn't put it quite as harshly as that, Jane darling," Lara dismissed. In a flurry of practised movements, she swept the hair up into a pony tail, her fingers gliding around on her daughter's translucent skin, "but I have to confess, thank goodness this house has long since been paid for, or else we would have to move into a ghastly little city house with all manner of neighbours around one, like fleas."

"Does that mean I can safely say we're rich? Hannah says there are no real rich people, only beggars and borrowers, and that anyway wanting to be rich is a sin, because the first shall be the last and the last shall be the first," she played with her fringe in the mirror. "Anyway, Rebecca told her to save all that preaching nonsense for those who didn't know better, and she said that Hannah was only trying to make up for with intelligence what she was lacking in beauty and success. Rebecca is in very pretty, you know, mother," Jane raised her chin proudly and looked down the length of her nose at her red lips. She looked a good while before realising that the soothing strokes across her scalp had stopped. Jane spun round.

"Mother?" her voice worried, "Why have you stopped? What's the matter, mother?"

Lara placed the hairbrush gently on the table. The ring she had chosen glimmered promisingly on her finger.

"Why does one stop anything at all, Jane?" she leant forward, caressed Jane's crown with her ear, and her eyes closed against the knot in her breasts as they breezed along her daughter's shoulders.

Their eyes met in the mirror.

"Jane, my darling," she stroked the pale neck, and caught a faint trace of her daughter's scent; a flowery, innocent scent on the point of turning. "One stops," she sighed, "because one must..."

"Jane!"

Mother and daughter spun round, alarmed.

"Oh, Rosemary!" Jane stumbled to her feet apologetically, her limbs confused, vaguely aware of some impropriety.

Rosemary was standing in the doorway, already dressed. Her eyes fired suspiciously from the one reddening face to the other.

"Hello Rosemary," said Lara, softly, and tied the belt of her dressing-gown tighter before clasping the two silk halves of cloth about her throat. "I just came in to brush Jane's hair for her. I suppose it's time I got dressed, too." She left Jane's side. Paused once she had got to the doorway.

Rosemary's eyes fell upon her mother's hand. Upon the ring. Upon the hardened circles inside her mother's dressing-gown. She looked away hastily.

"Anyway, it's lovely to have you both home again,"
she smiled weakly.

Neither of them looked at her.

Lara crept out of the room.

"What did she want?" said Rosemary after a long
while. After she had heard the quiet click of another door
closing. Her eyes alone ventured into the room. This had
been her room once. Now only Jane was allowed to be
here.

"What did she want, then?"

Her sister sat on the bed and placed her hands in her lap.
That deep and satisfying prickling of her scalp had gone.

"As she said," Jane replied. "She just wanted to brush
my hair. Has she never wanted to brush your hair,
Rosemary?"

"No," Rosemary lied. "I'll wait downstairs. Don't be
long."

"May I brush your hair, it's so lovely!" her mother
entered the room.

The girl was nervous. She perched on the chair and
shivered.

Her mother brushed and brushed. Her two girls had
lovely hair; beautiful, glossy, long, thick hair. Strong. Like
faith. She would always give them the chance to tell her
first. Always... So of course it had hurt to discover that
the child had preferred to lie.

"Close your eyes, darling..."

"Mama -"

"It's too late. Ssssh!" Her mother cooed. "Close
your eyes. And don't move. Not a hair."

It had sounded like someone eating a mouthful of
something crunchy. The thick red mass sank silently to

mother's feet, though a few strands managed to cling to her dressing-gown. Mother's hand lingered as she brushed them off.

Rosemary's eyes were wide open.

"Don't scream," said mother, and the voice seemed years away from the woman who was standing so close. "Don't... scream." Mother felt the young, blood-drained face quiver up to an uncontrollable flood of tears. "And don't cry, either," she said. Her voice no longer creaming over with that suppressed motherly enthusiasm, yet warm in another way; in a way which seemed to accept the happening of the inevitable; in a way which was relieved at finally being able to sweep fear aside. "I did ask you, Rosemary. I gave you the chance to tell me first." Lara's heavy sigh whisked a stolen red thread of hair from Rosemary's shoulder. "This is Jane's room now, Rosemary. You will have to move out to the north wing."

Somewhere behind her, layers and layers of pain, of shame, away, the child heard the footsteps withdraw to the door.

"Rosemary..."

The girl was staring quizzically at her new face; at the hair, hanging in limbo between her ear and shoulder, and she felt light. And cold.

"You are never to let your hair grow long again, Rosemary."

The door went, "Click."

She remembered counting the number of stairs when she was very young. And she remembered never coming to the same number. The stairs were playing with her she had thought then. Her mother had laughed at the proclamation, "Mama, I'm going to play with the stairs."

"Don't you mean *on* the stairs, Jane darling?"
No, Jane had insisted, stamping her little podgy foot, "I'm going to play with the stairs, Mama. *With!*" She scrambled up and down, holding onto the smoothly rounded banister pegs. Later, she would be big enough to let her hand breeze effortlessly along the deliciously polished wood which decked the pegs in a strong, graceful movement of mahogany sweeping through the heart of the house and curling to rest in the spacious main hall. Later still, standing at the top of the stairs, she would lay a ribbon on the hand-rest, animate it with a faint puff of her breath, and follow it with her eyes as it glided down and away, landing in a delicate pile of air-filled folds. Jane would then skip down the stairs after it, her head turned away from the pictures; those dark oil portraits staring down at her; a row of ugly, pinched women who didn't like her and wanted to get her.

"Papa," she declared some years later over lunch. The maid slid in and out like a secret, and removed the soup tureen in a well-oiled movement. "Do you know what, Papa?"

"What, Jane darling?" Papa was wearing a faint smile, put on as the maid went by. The maid could feel him, sitting there, smiling, his mind reclining on some delectable memory of her. Her feet hurried her into the kitchen.

When Jane was still very small, a visitor had exclaimed how pretty she was, and had bent down to ask her her name. Jane, taking her finger out of her mouth with a plop, had promptly replied, "Jane darling." The whole room had erupted into laughter, and Jane, confused, had run away in tears.

"Do you know what, Papa? The stairs are odd. I mean, They're an odd number."

Papa took a sip from a glass of water.

"That wouldn't surprise me, Jane darling," he straightened the napkin on his lap. "That would not surprise me in the least..."

His daughter didn't quite know what to make of this enigmatic rejoinder. She turned to her mother, whom she witnessed looking at Papa with cold contempt. She neither knew how or why, but in a flash, Jane knew that her mother belonged to those women on the stairs.

One of whom was Regina Morton. She hung at the foot of the stairs, as large as and as uncompromising as a solid oak door; the threshold between the higher and lower regions of Morton House. Solemn in black, Regina Morton's face was as stern as a rusted padlock, and the contours of her body melted mysteriously into the background. Only her face was light - luminous still - though the oil had hardened and cracked over the centuries.   Ugly, Jane had said, categorically. Lara had been quick to correct her.

"Regina Morton was not an ugly woman, Jane. She was simply painted by someone who misunderstood her. By someone who no doubt...no,"

Lara brushed a few strands of red hair from her daughter's face and tucked them lovingly behind the child's ear. The pang of guilt, that certain sense of unworthiness, had already begun to fade, and still, Lara preferred to fix her gaze on the child than on the portrait.

"This marvellous, this -" she searched for words, her eyes flitting about restlessly, "this *courageous* woman, far from being ugly, was simply painted by someone who was certainly," she laid a serious hand on Jane's shoulder, "*certainly* afraid of her," Lara straightened up and inhaled deeply.

Jane considered her mother rather beautiful, although she too, as young as she was, hadn't failed to notice the sad-lines that had crept together for comfort around her mother's large, hopeful eyes. That anyone should choose to refute such beauty was as incomprehensible as - as someone denying the deliciousness of sunshine. Now who should do that?

But Lara hadn't quite said all she had to say. She risked a glance at the portrait before sighing even more deeply, "Regina Morton... she was painted by a man. Who else..."

By a man, who else... Jane stood at the top of the stairs, and was suddenly afraid to go down. Rosemary was waiting in the courtyard. Her footsteps tramped up and down impatiently, and her voice rose haughtily to one of the hands. Rosemary didn't like to be kept waiting. Jane stood at the top of the stairs. And was afraid. Afraid of having to pass Regina Morton.

"Regina Morton?"

"Yes."

"Regina Morton?" Rosemary strode off. The crunching gravel soon gave way to yielding green. "What on earth am I supposed to know about Regina Morton? She's been dead for centuries."

Though Rosemary was merely three years older, Jane had sensed enormous changes. Everything about her sister now seemed so far away; the stepping stones of her development far too far apart to allow her sibling to spring across effortlessly and to fall, squealing, into her arms. Never, had Jane felt so alone. So stranded. They attended different schools and had their different girlfriends, not that this had stopped them from being the closest of sisters in the past. Rosemary, who would let Jane creep into her room and under her bedclothes so they could brush each other's hair and read stories together, now shook Jane off as though she were an over-eager puppy that had lost its appeal. At the dinner table, lately, Jane sometimes felt Rosemary's eyes boring into her; felt that cold glare pinching her maliciously, and she wondered what it was that she had done wrong. She couldn't shake off the feeling of being spied upon; Rosemary, her mother, both of them were watching her with disconcerting eagerness; watching and waiting for some new development. Hopping from one foot to the other, like excited canaries. Sitting in her room, at the mirror, her rope of hair brushed out for the night, Jane would sometimes be seized by panic. She wondered who that girl in the mirror might be and what it was that was expected of her. If only Rosemary would come and they could share beds again. But Rosemary never came. Not once. Jane plaited her hair together before climbing in between the starched sheets. *Why do things have to change?*

She ran along behind her elder sister who was storming away from the house with a tempo only rage could have incited. Rosemary's red shorn head bobbed along like some furious insect. *She isn't walking, either...* Jane thought, her plait slapping her back as she fought to keep pace, *she's kicking, and stamping, and snorting... she's flaring her nostrils at me, and she'd bite, too...*

Rosemary had stopped being kind to her, when? The day she had had to move out of Miss´ Room. The day she had cut her hair. How Jane had gasped at her cropped sister! How her focus spilled by the tears in her eyes!

"Rosemary!" she had screamed, running to her sister. "Why?" And Jane threw her arms about her sister. "Why?"

Rosemary had had to fight to keep her balance. To keep her own eyes dry. She pried herself from the arms flung around her neck, peeling back each finger with her own, then climbed free and brushed herself off. Brushed her sister's adoration off, as though it were the left-over yarn from an embroidery one had just finished and was glad to be able to finally put aside. She would not look, but she could feel Jane standing there; Jane's arms, her eyes, hanging in the air where they had been discarded. Poor little Jane. Poor, little Jane, but really, Rosemary was herself too wounded, too angry and too ashamed for apologies.

"Why? Why does one do anything at all?" she summoned up one of her mother's smiles. "Because one wants to. Or has to," then she disappeared for the rest of that day in her room. Her new room. Miss' Room was Jane's room now, and as Jane's arms drifted back to place, so came the notion that Rosemary's leaving was a very severe punishment for something Jane was too afraid to want to know.

"I want to know what it's all about!" Jane panted.

"What on earth are you talking about, child?" Rosemary tossed the insult behind her. Nor did she need to look over her shoulder to know that Jane had flinched. Their meeting only in the holidays did nothing to detract from the fact that they were still sisters - once even inseparable sisters - and if there was one thing sisters quickly learnt to do, their love for each other notwithstanding, then that was how best to hurt one another. Rosemary struck with precision, with skill, and did not bother herself with a glance to see if she had hit the mark.

"I'm not a child!" Jane retorted, "I'm thirteen years old! As old as you were when you had to move out!"
It was Rosemary's turn to flinch.

"As old as you were when you cut your hair!" Jane prodded deeper. "So, what's it all about? And this horrid doll's house? And Regina Morton?"

Rosemary knew that Regina Morton had had an affair with one of the hands, and that the two, having killed her husband, Harold Morton, had successfully managed to pass it off as a shooting accident. Five months later, Regina Morton bore her dead husband a daughter. He would have been displeased; an ugly little child with hair as red as his own; a daughter at that. His wife, however, considering herself as thus having fulfilled her role, went back to her own life. And her lover. It had become common knowledge. Common, scandalous, wicked knowledge. With an alacrity that could only stem from an unpleasant consciousness of one's own misdemeanours, society scraped Regina Morton from its meeting places; its parties; its punctilious happenings. She is said not to have cared a hoot and, decades later, to have died not altogether happy, but, in her own words, true to herself. There had even been talk of taking her daughter away. That a woman of such - *inclinations* - could not be a fit mother. Would only contaminate her daughter by her unmentionable example. There was talk. Much talk, and Isabella Morton was pursued by the castigating whispers her entire life, and by her own misguided shame. Her mother had sought for further uproar by her will, in which was stated that Morton House be passed onto a female heir. There were first cousins and second cousins and uncles enough, rubbing their hands together, perfuming their hair and only too eager to slip a frail band of gold on her daughter's finger, yet Regina had her own designs. Morton would belong to Isabella, and Isabella was to pass it onto her daughter, and her daughter to her daughter, handing it down from woman to woman. Forever. Only so would Regina be able to save her line from the toil of slavery, sycophancy and prostitution to which all women are subjected, to a greater or lesser degree. In vain did her lawyer try everything in his power to bring her back to her senses.

"Do stop flapping, you stupid man," Regina Morton is said to have advised him with a gentle, playful curl of her full lips. "The shoe is not as comfortable on the other foot, now is it?" Thereupon she took the document from under his nose, signed it, blew her signature dry and asked him to leave her premises.

"Give my regards to that admirable young nephew of yours. Reginald, if my memory serves me well?"

"Edward," her lawyer corrected, pulling sternly at the hem of his waistcoat.

"Yes," Regina had been smiling for quite a while. "Give him my regards."

"Regina Morton... I think she's a great-great-grandmother or something. Mother's side."

"What do you know about her?"

"No more than you do."

"You're lying!"

"Why should I?"

"Oh, Rosemary!"

"What do you want from me, Jane?" Rosemary span round all of a sudden, her hands on her hips. "Just what is it you want?"

"Rosemary..." at first taken aback by the ferocity of her sister's response, Jane now cautioned a step forward, "why did you really cut -" but before she could finish, Rosemary had bolted away, leaving her to crumble to her knees, exasperated, her face red from exertion. "It wasn't you, was it?" she stretched her legs out, looked beyond the hill down which her sister had disappeared, and resigned herself to spending the morning out there alone. "But why don't you like me anymore? You can have Miss' Room, if that's what it's about. I don't like it anyway. Oh, Rosemary!"

Morton House. A house of many rooms. Handsome rooms slenderly windowed, maintained by a tatty frill of faithful servants. An elegant stone building at the end of a long avenue of poplars whistling a greeting as one rode by; fingers turning and glistening in the wind. Admirable property, Morton House. Its green fields breezed out like an exquisite roll of cloth fluttering in the air, inhaling light, and for a second, engulfing all in colour; in texture, through whose fibres that world out there seemed beautiful. And possible. And yours, for a moment, before the colours sank to your fingers and enticed you to feel. Morton House. The women draped the possession around their slender shoulders.

The men came.

"It's a girl," she said as she carried the slippery arrival over to a deep bowl of gently warmed water on a chest of drawers by the window.

"A girl, did you say?" She was not a midwife, but mother had insisted; her, and only her. Mother was ready and, in her presence, relaxed. Giving birth, their most intimate encounter.

"Yes, a girl. I daren't say 'the Master' shan't be too pleased... Next time..."

"Her name is Victoria."

"She is as beautiful as her mother."

Mother smiled, her eyes deeply fixed on the woman bringing her her child. "Very well. Victoria Isabella."

Little Miss had an awful temper. A will of her own inside that shock of red hair. By all accounts she was every bit like Ma'am's grandmother, Regina Morton. Little Miss Amanda bit her nurse on the finger. The master banished her to her room in the East Wing.

Harold, pleased with his recent acquisition, looked up from his book with a satisfied smile as she came in.

"Have you finished inspecting your new home, Regina?"

"Yes, Harold, I have."

Her husband resumed his reading. Expected his young wife to leave.

"Whom did that doll-house in the East Wing belong to? Your mother, by any chance?"

"Doll-house? Oh, you mean the house of dolls! I really couldn't tell you. As far as I know, it's been here longer than anyone here can even remember. Or cares to. I've never seen the thing myself. That was mother's room, as a child. Miss´ Room, they call it. And men don't go there." He chuckled dryly. "I was always in the South Wing."

"It's so fascinating!" Regina bubbled into the room. "It's full of miniature dolls! Lace up to the neck and hems down to the toes, you know how women used to dress before, and they're wearing the most curious of smiles, but, you know, Harold," and she wanted to add, "darling", but did not dare to, "the house is definitely not a replica of Morton, so someone must have brought it along with her at some point." She was standing a pace or two behind him by now, having inched her way forward with each enthusiastic word. Regina would have liked to place a hand on his shoulder, to spin him round and let him see how delighted the find had made her. Only, could she show him her delight without also revealing her fear? For there was also something frightful about the house of dolls. Familiar, in a way it could not possibly be, given that she had never seen the object before. Unparcelling Morton House proved exhilarating. A never-ending birthday for a woman as young and as gay as Regina. *I'm Regina of Morton House... Regina... of Morton House*, she was singing to herself happily as she approached Miss' Room. She eased the door open, her breath held. Her eyes were wide and expectant and her hand was moist around the cold, iron handle. The doll-house nestled between the two imposing windows which appeared to be keeping watch over it. It was the first thing one saw. Regina hurried into the room with a startled cry and fell to her knees before it. She looked hastily over her shoulder; wanted, on the one hand, to get up and close the door, at best to lock it, and on the other, she wished to remain as she was, on her knees, breathless before this altar of female childhood fantasy. Gently, she opened its doors, eased back the plush red drapes. In that instant, when that deep richness of cloth touched her fingers, indecision made her remain - she did not know how long - in that position. Lost. Her hand just inside the door...

She had hurried down the stairs. An inexplicable sense of guilt mingling with fear, yet Regina was outrageously happy.

"Harold?" His hair was already beginning to thin. An area the size of a saucer. If she were to lean forward, she would be able to touch his shoulder. "Harold?" she repeated in her inexperience at deciphering his various silences.

"Regina, my dearest," his eyes were closed. His voice strained. "Can't you see that I'm reading?"

Mama lay in bed, half dead, her skin as thin, as watery as her eyes, whose lids were sealed by a blue line of sleep-denying pain. The nurse who had been sitting by her bedside ever since the ordeal was over, rose silently to her feet and rearranged the heavily embroidered covers around her patient's hot neck. Outside, the winter, banished from the room by thick, dark drapes, crept around the other entries to the house and stole in through an opened kitchen window, where the servants went about their chores in subdued manoeuvres.

It was a boy. The boy was dead. Dead, and rotting, and trapped inside that narrow passage-way, for hours, whilst his mother had screamed and thrashed. Unprepared for any such complications, the doctor had sent the nurse to fetch the cook, who had bustled up the stairs importantly and thrown a mild glance at the master of the house as he paced up and down in the Main Hall. But the child was dead. A boy. Papa snatched his shotgun and marched off to the stables.

"Go outside and play, Lara," my nurse said. "Go upstairs for one of your dolls and play with her under the chestnut tree beyond the hill."

The vicar had arrived. A sinewy, sharp-eyed man, who uttered deep, solemn words, and waited impatiently for Mama's blued eyes to take note of his presence. She should rest, he said. Rest, get well again as soon as she could in order to resume her duties as a wife. And mother. Her husband was a good, God-fearing man. He deserved a son. Therefore, rest.

Had she decided upon a name for the child?
Mama's head nodded weakly.

And what was that name?
I heard my nurse calling after me, "Lara? Lara? Don't go further than you know you are allowed to!" I kicked that horrid doll ahead of me and ran. Away from my pain. Only dolls are always happy. Away from mama's pain.
Mama was simply too weak.

I beg your pardon? The vicar spoke somewhat loudly, thrusting his head at the woman's face.
Amanda closed her eyes and licked her lips, "Victor."

"Rosemary!" she had heard Jane scream. What would Rosemary say? Would she tell the truth? Did she even know the truth? She wondered if Jane would come to her for an explanation. Lara decided to call their wedding photographer in London, to see if he knew anyone who could do her in oil. It was time. The thought had come to her that, far from being a permanent, uninterrupted flow, time was rather like a pack of cards; clear, defined slices one could shuffle, play with. Win. Or lose. As the scissors bit their way through that awesome mass of hair, she realised that her opponent had a stronger hand. The slice fell. Rosemary would have to be told about Regina Morton. It was time. Lara would have herself done in oil, and she hoped the portraitist would not be afraid of her. Hoped he would not allow his fear to seep into the canvas. She was Lara of Morton House. He would have heard the stories. Would no doubt be afraid. Or could it be that she was afraid of him? She did not know; all she knew was that an element of fear was never to be discounted whenever the eyes of these two arch-rivals meet. It was time. Regina had waited too long. She should have had herself committed to perpetuity with a triumphant glow in her eyes. Lara would not make the same mistake, at least she hoped that she would not, although the necessity of that morning's activity had delivered a staggering blow. She had to have herself painted at once, whilst there was still a faint glow of radiance about her. It was time.

"Your bath is ready, Ma'am," a voice said on the other side of the door.

"Thank you. I'll bathe myself this time. You may go now."

Looking in the mirror, Lara asked herself, "Am I beautiful?" Her husband would have said yes, once upon a time, not that his opinion mattered any more. And yet she hadn't changed. Did that mean that beauty was more conviction than fact? She concluded that it did. Furthermore, as a woman, she had as much right to admiration as a man, who would have her believe that he gave her all, when in truth he was bent on shovelling all the attention for himself. Even his choice of wife, what was that if not mere strategy, aimed at securing the praise of those by whom he essentially wished to be praised. By other men, no less. *And we women bicker and twitter and preen ourselves under the delusion that we are more than an adornment,* she ran her fingers briskly through her short hair. It was all too disgusting. All too much effort, when so many were bound to wake up one day, look at the face next to their own, and be overcome with the unshakeable conviction of having made the biggest mistake of their life. And what for? For adornments, of which they themselves were the biggest one. They would have to learn to play. To shuffle and cut the pack. To become adroit, and yet remain faithful to the callings of their own impulses. To wash themselves of this whorish dependence.

Yes, her chin tilted proudly towards the glass. Yes, she *was* beautiful. Lara let her robe fall to her feet, then admired herself; her somewhat thin arms, her tired pockets of flesh, her stretchmarks.

"Yes. I *am* beautiful."

She resolved to visit her lover that evening. Tell of the new development with Rosemary. Lara slid into the hot, scented water, and her daughter's hair, that of it which had managed to find refuge inside her dressing-gown, floated away from her body - her neck, her breasts, her thighs - and settled on the surface in a red powder.

Jane has been in Miss' Room for nearly two years. Lara is pleased. And grateful. Jane is beautiful. Her hair is beautiful.

Rosemary says she wants to go to college, and that she will never marry. Her father said that that would be an awful loss. Lara chose to keep her opinion on the matter to herself. She is standing by the window, and can see her two girls walking up the hill. They appear to be in deep conversation. She wonders who the initiator of the conversation was, and what it is they are talking about.

Rosemary is at peace with herself. Lara is glad. She rests her hand on the roof of the miniature house to her right. Strokes it lovingly. Jane has turned around, she looks down the hill, and sees her home, like a toy, at her feet, and a speck of green in the window is waving at her. Jane waves back, both arms raised high above her head, like a person in peril, but Lara knows she is safe. For the time being. Lara waves, and smiles, and as she raises her hand in the air, the scissors in the one pocket brush against her leg. In the other, the hairbrush is warm and full. Rosemary does not look round.

Lara is thankful that Rosemary's nightmares have come to an end; the months of fear in which that cold metal blade in her pocket tormented her daughter's sleep. She is sorry. Rosemary preferred not to comment on the portrait. Jane said how lovely it was, that mother was somehow much better than the others. Father excused himself from the table.

All the dolls are still there. Lara straightens up and gives a sigh of relief. Their curious, eternal smile, their trustful eyes - is it not strange that their effect had in no way diminished over all those years?

Jane and Rosemary have disappeared over the brow of the hill. Lara is not afraid. She has locked the door so no one can get in or out.

Her mother had locked the door so no one could get in or out.

Grandmother had locked the door so no one could get in or out.

Great-grandmother, too, had locked the door so no one could get in or out.

Great-great-grandmother had sat by this same window, the metal cold against her skin, and her rage would not cool.

Great-great-grandfather had slipped the key into a leather pouch about his neck, and had ridden off for days and days.

The dolls are as beautiful as ever. Their smile, *timeless.*

Papermate

You need not fear me anymore

Or rather,
you need not fear *her* anymore:.
for she has gone
she won't
trouble you from now on:
I have put her back to where she was
before you came along.

I thought there would be
room
for her
in my life

I realize now that there still isn't
if I am to continue
the life I lead now

Better keep her under lock
and
key…

Sounds
as though I am
talking about some
hideous monster
doesn't it:
something
horribly dangerous that
no-one

seems able to cope with
and not
that I am talking about
something
natural; something
as innocent
as curious...

Something legitimate

Anyhow
back home she goes
where we can both live
safe from harm.

If only
it would not cost me
so much
effort
to keep her
in her
place...

Never have I been so
tired
in all my life -
drained
in the middle
of the day so that my only option
was to lay down
my head
and
close my eyes to
such insuperable

inexplicable
fatigue

Until my mind walked the
bridge between my
exhaustion
and the
effort I expended daily to
suppress
the Woman
in me.

And there I was
fearing another pregnancy!

In a sense, I am;
with child, though she will
never be born;
never grow to be strong
and
independent
or the source of pleasure to my eye...

My secret she will forever remain –
my Jew in the attic:
I look in from time
to time -
she may stay
provided she keeps a
low
profile...

And when no-one's about, I stay
a little longer -

move a little closer;
strike up a conversation
which is always amazing

Why, I ask myself
why should anyone fear
something so wonderful;
why should she
have to
hide?

And in moments of intense
defiance
I refuse to hide her:

I let her come
out

And she may live:

On paper.

View

Be they closed
or opened
my eyes
they see you;
see the look you
throw me like a
sumptuous gown
shivering
from my shoulders
at the touch…

Boy Queen

In the morning when I coyed your skin
it felt
like velvet fur
your Nubian lips glossed
by the yolk
of the rising sun.

You made me sigh
I made you
cry...
you showed me all your graces
your fire and desire
you made me sigh...
I
made you cry but
kissed such
tears
away.

Wearing on mine
your pith turned child
beautiful bright boy
my prince
some being born out of the
queen in flight
dark
as the night was warm
was thinly clothed
with shy whispers
crumpled by the
wrath of sheets.

You showed me the
soft side
the
dark side
showed me
the wildcat
poised
beneath that
African pride…
disclosed your
every shade
of woman
to my man
who kissed away
lone tears
who cradled that
fragility till anxiety had
faded
bodies cascading
in moments
stretched
to years.

Bernstein

I want to do to you
as the sunlight to the soles of the leaves
as the night to our sighs
before joy inebriates us to sleep.

I want to do to you
as birdsong, tossed recklessly to the arms of the sky
as the brook to the pebbles' moss
furled at her feet.

I want to do to you
as the forgotten strand of hair to the skin
as the horizon laced to our deepest wish
galloping, galloping.

I want to do to you
as the murderous downpour to the
newborn petal
as the meteor
searing the flesh
of the violet night
as the beast to the virgin…

I am the thunder to your stars
I am the blossom
I am the rock.

I am the silence of your heartbeat
stilled by the temple of our love.

I am the fire to your fears
I am the church-bell to your devout ears.

I am the bud
thrusting to life
in your sunshine.

I am that moment:
precious
frozen green.

I am the valet to your needs.

I am you, you are me
in a pyre, the debris of our limbs
fanned by our blessed mournful cries.

I am the musk to your rose
pining my name when I have
gone
drinking my smell as it hovers
on in a languid mist
over your golden cornfield.

I am the joyous fly
cradled
in your silken
thread.

I am ocean
I am language
I the vagabond
scouring your territory
for I want to do to you:

as the butterfly to the heart of the child

as the salt to the pearls in her sea

as the candle to the night

as sunlight to Bernstein.

Perfume

I love the smell of you. After you had gone the other day, I refused to wash myself. She came home later, wanting, the usual, but I couldn't touch her. She slept on her side of the bed and I on mine. (Yes, she recollected, he had pulled her to that side of the bed...) I on mine, enveloped in the odour of your juice and sweat. She? She washes at least ten times a day, how's a man supposed to get excited if he doesn't have the smell of you in his nose? We wash far too often. Should only wash when we really need to. You should get Him not to wash for a while so he stinks of man, then you give him a royal blow job, he'll spray like a whale, I swear.

You, you smell fantastic, your tight, juicy *foufoun*. I read a book once, in French it's called *Le Nez*; The Nose. Know it? It's about a man who kills virgins so he can use their odour to produce the ultimate perfume. That's one crazy shit, but I understand him. When I sniff my fingers, hhmm, I smell you. I run my fingers under my nose right in front of her, and remember you. I'm not going to wash that bedsheet. Going to keep it somewhere safe so I can smell you when I want to.

My wedding day, right? First marriage, and I'm at my in-laws. The future bride and her parents had gone to the hairdresser's. We were celebrating the wedding at home, so the bride's family had asked a neighbour to help out with serving the guests. She was a young, unattractive girl. Come and help me, come and scrub my back for me, I called out to her. She came and scrubbed my back. Thick as a plank, she was. Get in the tub... She was a country lass and she really did smell of c(o)untry. I moved my head down there to get a whiff of

168

her, but believe me, one whiff was enough, even for a man like me. We had a good shag right there in the bathtub. Then I got dressed and got married.

In the village of my childhood, you wore your underwear for the whole week and washed at the weekend. (Girls as well?) of course girls as well! The air was rank by Friday! And our *culottes* yellow up the front, brown up the back. (You look happy at the recollection of it...) of course I was happy! Life was simple, but sweet... This is the smell I have in my nostrils till today. This smell, this innocence, of unwashed sex.

In the old days, all the children slept in one bed. Of course there was incest going on. So what? You always hear about fathers raping their daughters. Now you listen to me. Half the time, it's not rape at all. Those girls want it. They want to make the experience, and then when they get jealous of their fathers, they accuse him of rape to get their own back, and the poor bastard ends up in prison. We were kids, but we weren't doing anything abnormal, see?. Kids are like this. Kids are sexual beings, too.

Boys were trying it out amongst themselves as well, of course they were. I saw my brother get buggered by the boy next door. He was a good bit older than us, and he would often come over and sleep at our place on a Saturday night. Once I heard these noises coming from my brother's bedroom. I went in and flicked on the light. My brother was on his knees, this other big boy had him by the hips and was giving him a royal humping. I think I said something like; you dirty bastards, that's what girls are for! I think I also grabbed something and beat my brother across the backside with it. He knows I saw him, though we've never openly spoken about it. See, it was just like that, and do you think things have changed? Are you saying that I come from a family of mental cases? (So, who was humping you...?) I'll tell you one thing, it doesn't smell the same...

I am as I am
And it's right that way
What more do you want
What more must I say...

Credo

Desire -
suspended
between my fears;
graceful as the exhale of blue-grey smoke
so full of promise, so able to be
anything, able to go
anywhere
before it vanishes
before its sole souvenir is an odour
lingering
awaiting my courage to claim it as my flesh
and blood…

Can it be my goal
should it be
to transcend my physical needs
to robe myself in an orange cloth
and take
to the streets
with my bowl?

I am human -
I am woman -
I beg of You

Flesh

Not dust

Not yet…

www.ingramcontent.com/pod-product-compliance
Lightning Source LLC
Chambersburg PA
CBHW020337260626
47156CB00004B/1565